The **HOLIDAY HONEYMOON** fun continues this month, when Gulliver's Travels employee **LUCY FALCO** rekindles the flame with **CHRISTOPHER BANKS**.

So if you loved the earlier HOLIDAY HONEYMOON books—or even if you missed them—you're sure to enjoy this sensuous, fun-filled romance by award-winning author Carole Buck.

* * *

Praise for Carole Buck's earlier Desire miniseries WEDDING BELLES...

"...In *Annie Says I Do*...readers will appreciate how Ms. Buck skillfully turns a lifelong friendship into a passionate love affair."

"...*Peachy's Proposal* [is] a scrumptious confection of a delight... Ms. Buck...creates a keeper for your bookshelf."

"[In]...*Zoe and the Best Man*...Ms. Buck gifts us with a clever, witty love story with oodles of warm sensuality and touching emotion."
—Melinda Helfer, *Romantic Times*

Dear Reader,

Welcome to a wonderful new year at Silhouette Desire! Let's start with a delightfully humorous MAN OF THE MONTH by Lass Small—*The Coffeepot Inn*. Here, a sinfully sexy hero is tempted by a virtuous woman. He's determined to protect her from becoming the prey of the local men—*and* he's determined to win her for himself!

The HOLIDAY HONEYMOONS miniseries continues this month with *Resolved To (Re)Marry* by Carole Buck. Don't miss this latest installment of this delightful continuity series!

And the always wonderful Jennifer Greene continues her STANFORD SISTERS series with *Bachelor Mom*. As many of you know, Jennifer is an award winner, and this book shows why she is so popular with readers and critics alike!

Completing the month are a new love story from the sizzling pen of Beverly Barton, *The Tender Trap;* a delightful Western from Pamela Macaluso, *The Loneliest Cowboy;* and something a little bit different from Ashley Summers, *On Wings of Love.*

Enjoy!

Lucia Macro

Senior Editor

Please address questions and book requests to:
Silhouette Reader Service
U.S.: 3010 Walden Ave., P.O. Box 1325, Buffalo, NY 14269
Canadian: P.O. Box 609, Fort Erie, Ont. L2A 5X3

CAROLE BUCK
RESOLVED TO (RE)MARRY

SILHOUETTE *Desire*®

Published by Silhouette Books

America's Publisher of Contemporary Romance

SILHOUETTE BOOKS

ISBN 0-373-76049-3

RESOLVED TO (RE)MARRY

CAROLE BUCK

is a television news writer and movie reviewer who lives in Atlanta. She is single and her hobbies include cake decorating, ballet and traveling. She collects frogs, but does not kiss them. Carole says she's in love with life; she hopes the books she writes reflect this.

Prologue

It was the final night of December, and the former Lucia Annette Falco and her new husband, Christopher Dodson Banks, were too intoxicated to fully understand what they were doing.

Their euphoric deficit of comprehension had nothing to do with alcohol. The only liquor either of them had imbibed on this New Year's Eve was a few pro forma sips of champagne at their wedding reception. If they'd been tested, they would have registered stone-cold sober.

So why were Chris's normally steady limbs as wobbly as a wino's as he stood in the center of the hotel suite where he intended to consummate the marriage vows he'd uttered with such solemnity earlier that evening?

And why was Lucy feeling as giggly and giddy as a prom queen at a frat-house keg party as she anticipated doing exactly the same thing?

To put it simply—or not so simply, as things turned out—the newly wed Mr. and Mrs. Banks were drunk with love.

And dreams.

His dreams about her.

Her dreams about him.

Their dreams . . . about themselves and their future together.

The fact that only a few of these dreams had been clearly articulated by either party—and that several of the more crucial unspoken ones seemed to be downright contradictory—was something neither the bride nor the groom had taken time to consider.

Such was the nature of their mutual intoxication.

Lucy melted against Chris with a purr of delight as he gathered her tenderly into his arms. She clung to him, nuzzling at his chest. Breathing in deeply, she savored the subtle spice of his cologne and the potent hint of natural male musk that lay beneath it.

She adored the way her new husband smelled.

And tasted.

And felt.

She was nuts about the way he looked, too.

Funny. She'd grown up assuming that when she finally surrendered to the urge to merge, her mate would be some hunky Mediterranean-type male. And why not? The vast majority of the guys she'd gone out with had been cast from the same dark-eyed, dark-haired, olive-complected mold. They'd sported tight jeans and black leather jackets. They'd also—with the notable exception of Chachi Palucci, who'd tried to impress her with plagiarized poetry—been prone to flexing their well-developed pecs in an effort to incite her admiration.

Whereas Chris . . .

Well, the man to whom she'd given herself in every sense of the phrase had hazel eyes. His thick, straight hair was a sun-gilded caramel brown. Although his skin had been burnished by years of tennis, skiing and sailing, it was pale in the places the sun had never touched.

The bulk of his well-tailored wardrobe came from Brooks Brothers, Paul Stuart and Ralph Lauren. He wore leather on his feet and around his narrow waist, and that was it. He was tall—six feet to her own five-five—and built along lean, angular lines. While he was not the kind of man who indulged in false modesty, neither was he inclined to strut his stuff.

In short, Christopher Dodson Banks was not her type. No way. No how.

Or so Lucia Annette Falco would have sworn, until the sultry Saturday night when her gaze connected with his for the first time.

He had been checking out her chest when she registered his existence in the world. No big deal, really. She'd blossomed from soda-straw skinniness to a C cup the summer before she entered seventh grade, and she'd been getting ogled ever since.

Although she didn't particularly relish the attention her bosom attracted, Lucy had come to terms with it. She'd also discovered that the apparently genetically ingrained male tendency to assume that a woman's IQ was inversely proportional to her bra size could be turned to her advantage. She didn't play dumb. She had too much self-respect to resort to that kind of ploy. But there were situations in which she consciously refrained from flaunting her brains up front.

The few genuinely offensive members of the opposite sex she encountered—specifically, the jerks who grabbed without asking permission and who couldn't seem to grasp the concept that *no* meant *no,* not *maybe* or *take me*—she left to the not-so-tender mercies of her widowed father, three unmarried brothers, four uncles and ten male cousins. It wasn't that she didn't believe herself capable of fending off lechers. Quite the contrary. But as the only female Falco of her generation, she believed it behooved her to offer the men in her family the opportunity to defend her honor—and vent what she considered potentially dangerous buildups of excess testosterone—every now and then.

It was for her own peace of mind, really. As long as her *mucho macho* relatives were preoccupied with protecting her, they weren't going to have the time or energy to embroil themselves in any really serious trouble.

The tawny-haired stranger had lifted his gray-green eyes to her coffee-bean-brown ones a second or two after she glanced in his direction and became aware of his unabashed appraisal of her T-shirted breasts. She'd intended to blow him off like lint, for a variety of reasons, not the least of which was that she was sweating like a pig—thanks to her brothers' spectacularly inept efforts at air-conditioning repair—and didn't feel like being gawked at by some preppie-style prince who obviously didn't belong in Falco's Pizzeria. But as their gazes collided and locked, she'd felt a surge of attraction so powerful that she gasped aloud and grabbed for the side of the cash register she'd been tending for nigh on eight hours.

She'd tried to turn away, but found herself unable to do so. Her pulse had kicked like a chorus line. Her stomach had fluttered wildly. Nothing she'd experienced with any of the long line of neighborhood guys she'd dated during the five years since she'd celebrated her sweet sixteenth had prepared her for such a primal response.

Her ogler had flushed, obviously embarrassed. Obviously affected, too.

And then, astonishingly, he'd smiled at her.

It hadn't been one of those hey-baby-I'm-so-sexy grins she was accustomed to fielding from the local lotharios. Rather, it had been a quirking of flexible male lips, punctuated by a glint of even white teeth.

There'd been a trace of surprise in the expression. As though the smile represented a surrender to impulse by someone not usually given to succumbing to hormonally generated whim.

Lucy had reciprocated. Briefly. Breathlessly. If Chris had blinked, he probably would have missed it.

Despite the fact that she'd been accused—not completely without justification, she was willing to concede—of being a tease by several of the neighborhood Romeos, she hadn't been trying to be coy. Her control over her facial muscles had simply been too iffy for her to attempt a full-scale smile.

Lucia Annette Falco had not been hunting for a husband the day twenty-four-year-old Christopher Dodson Banks walked into her family's restaurant. She'd hoped to make a happy marriage eventually, of course. But not until she'd proven herself. By herself. To herself. For herself. And *not* until she'd firmly established her emotional and economic independence from her family.

She'd never imagined herself tying the knot while she was still two semesters away from earning her bachelor's degree in business administration. And even if she had, she *certainly* never would have envisioned a scenario in which the cause of her decision to reroute—some might suggest derail—her professional ambitions would be an Ivy League-educated lawyer who was the scion of one of Chicago's most prominent families!

Lucy's breath hitched in her throat as she suddenly recalled the disapproving expression she'd glimpsed on her new mother-in-law's perfectly made-up face as she and Chris departed for their honeymoon. She quickly shoved the memory aside. She'd find a way to deal with Elizabeth Banks, she assured herself. But not on this, the first night of her married life.

"I can't believe we actually did it," she whispered, scarcely realizing that she'd spoken aloud. The enormity of the commitment she'd made washed over her like a wave. For a moment, she felt as though she might drown.

"Well, we did, sweetheart." Chris hugged Lucy close, pressing his lips against the crown of her head. He inhaled sharply. The scent of a fresh floral perfume—and of warm feminine flesh—hazed his nostrils. Desire swirled through him like a zephyr. "You and me. Together. In front of a huge horde of witnesses."

"I *told* you I had a lot of relatives." There was an apology implicit in her soft voice. And an edge of defensiveness, too. The potentially troubling implications of both were lost in the rush of sensation unleashed by the stroking search of her hands.

"True," Chris acknowledged thickly, plucking the pins from her hair and scattering them on the floor. Lucy's family—boisterously affectionate, abundantly extended, the antithesis of his own limited network of blood kin—was something he envied her. Still, there had been more than a couple of instances during this evening's nuptial festivities when he found himself growing irritated by the number of guests who seemed to believe themselves entitled to lay claim to his bride's undivided attention. "But having to face all of them in the same place at the same time was a little overwhelming."

"Overwhelming," Lucy repeated in an odd tone, then shivered ardently as he finessed the nerve-rich skin of her nape. "I know ... what you mean."

Perhaps she did. Perhaps she didn't. Chris decided that it wasn't particularly important at this particular time. What mattered right now was that, after too many hours of being forced to share her, he finally had the woman he'd promised to love and honor as long as they both should live all to himself.

Was it selfish to want her so exclusively? he asked himself, unzipping Lucy's dress and sliding it off her smooth-skinned shoulders. She accommodated his efforts with a provocative little shimmy, then began undoing the buttons on the front of his shirt. Was it wrong to resent her seemingly endless interest in other people's problems?

Maybe, he conceded, sucking in his breath as he felt the delicate rake of fingernails against his hair-whorled chest. But it also struck him as being profoundly human.

They kissed again. Chris feathered his mouth back and forth, deepening the intimacy of the caress by carefully calibrated increments. Lucy's lips grew pliant, then parted. He eased his tongue between them, absorbing his bride's languid sigh of pleasure with a throaty invocation of her name.

She was so...*different*... from the kind of woman he—to say nothing of his parents, friends and professional colleagues—had expected he'd one day woo and wed. Not just in appearance. But in upbringing and outlook, as well.

This had unsettled Chris at the start of their relationship, and he'd tried to go slowly because of it. He hadn't doubted Lucy. He'd doubted himself.

He was self-aware enough to recognize that he wasn't—and probably never would be—entirely comfortable with the unearned privileges and unavoidable responsibilities that went with being the sole heir to the Banks family fortune. He'd needed to be certain that his desire to get involved with Lucia Annette Falco wasn't the manifestation of some long-deferred impulse toward rebelling against his birthright.

It had taken a fair amount of soul-searching, but he'd finally satisfied himself that his feelings were not the product of a postadolescent identity crisis. Which had been terrific, up to a point. Unfortunately, all the clumsy scrabbling around in his psyche hadn't help him figure out why he was drawn so intensely to a young woman with whom, by most objective standards, he seemed to have very little in common.

He'd replayed over and over again that first, heady moment when his eyes had connected with Lucy's, attempting to make sense of his instantaneous hunger for her. While Chris was no stranger to physical passion, he'd never before encountered a female who could make his mouth go dry and his palms start to sweat simply by *looking* at him. He'd eventually abandoned his quest for a rational explanation of what had happened, deciding that he'd probably have better luck trapping a lightning bolt between his hands during a thunderstorm.

The woman with whom he'd tumbled so precipitately in love was neither classically beautiful nor all-American cute. Her brows were too strongly marked, her jawline was too stubbornly angled and her gaze was too direct to qualify her for inclusion the latter category. As for the former—well, her nose missed being aristocratic by several significant millimeters, while her lush-lipped mouth was a degree or so off plumb and bracketed by dimples.

The thing was, Chris hadn't registered a single one of these flaws—if flaws they were—the first time he saw his future wife. Nor had he stopped to question why, after years of squiring lithesome blue-eyed blond debutantes, he'd suddenly found himself bewitched by a voluptuous brunette cashier at a pizzeria.

It had been her smile that initially snagged his attention. He'd seen her flash it at a slick-looking character in sunglasses and felt a strange stab to the heart. A surge of possessiveness had swept through him. He'd wanted that frank, feisty and oh-so-feminine expression directed at *him*—not some other guy.

After her smile, he'd focused on her skin. He'd longed to touch it. To taste it. To discover whether it carried the flavor, as well as the look, of sweet cream and sun-ripened apricots.

Her hair had compelled his senses, too. He'd yearned to free it from its haphazard ponytail and run his fingers through the long espresso-colored strands. To bury his face in the glossy tumble and breathe in its dusky fragrance.

As for the issue of when he'd noticed her breasts and exactly what he'd felt the urge to do with *them*—

"Mmm..." Lucy leaned back against the supportive circle of her new husband's arms, her loosened tresses shifting against her shoulder blades. She was hazily aware that she was ahead—or was it actually behind?—in the disrobing process. While she was down to a pair of pale silk stockings and a few fragile of pieces of lace-trimmed lingerie, Chris was still fully clad from the waist down.

"Mmm, indeed," he concurred, his normally cool eyes sparking emerald green and topaz gold from beneath partially lowered lids. Their expression was very focused. Almost fierce. His hands drifted down her back, curving seductively against her bottom. The warmth of his palms penetrated the fine fabric of her panties, kindling a melting heat between her thighs.

A tremor of uniquely feminine anticipation skittered through Lucy's nervous system. She shifted her hips, conscious of the thrusting rise of Chris's masculinity. She watched his nostrils flare on an abrupt exhalation of breath. A rush of color darkened the skin over his cheekbones. A thrilling sense of power—familiar in some ways, but far too new to be taken for granted—suffused her.

Although she hadn't reached age twenty-one untouched or ignorant about the facts of life, Christopher Dodson Banks was the only lover she'd ever had. They'd begun sleeping together two months after their first date. In some ways, she'd been more of the aggressor on that initial occasion than he.

Which was not to imply that he'd been passive. Indeed not. Although reticent about public displays of physical affection, Chris was intensely passionate in private. Making love with him was...well, it was a far cry from the wham-bam-in-the-back-seat encounters she'd heard about in the girls' rest room! He was inventive. Uninhibited. And unwaveringly intent on ensuring that what was good for him was even better for her.

"You're kidding me, Luce," her maid-of-honor-to-be, Tina Roberts, had said one night about six weeks ago. They'd been sharing confidences and cannolis after a long day of shopping for her trousseau. Tina, who'd gone all the way and then some her freshman year of high school, was the only one of Lucy's girlfriends who knew she'd been a virgin until Chris. Tina had also had a fair amount to say on the subject of how dangerous it could be for a girl to fall in love with the guy to whom she gave her physical innocence. "Without being *asked?*"

Lucy had fiddled with her pastry, wondering whether she'd been too forthcoming. "He said he enjoyed it because I...enjoy...it."

"He wasn't just trying to get you to—"

"*No,* Teen." The answer had been quick and unequivocal. It hadn't mattered that her companion was immensely more experienced than she. She'd felt very, very sure of her answer. "Chris isn't like that."

Tina had tapped her flashily manicured nails on the edge of the table at which they were sitting, an oddly wistful look flitting across her face. Finally she'd heaved a long-drawn-out sigh and observed, "I guess that old line about still waters running deep is true, huh? I mean, I'm not blind to your fiancé's appeal, hon. He's cute. He's classy. And even though I've never seen him do anything more than hold your hand, I can tell he's crazy for you. Still. I *never* would have pegged him as a tiger in the sack."

Lucy rose on tiptoe, brushing her mouth against Chris's. Their lips caught and clung, the caress escalating from airy to erotic in the space of a few increasingly frantic heartbeats.

"I love you, Chris," she whispered fervently. "I love you so much."

"I love you, too, Lucy," he answered, then bent and lifted her. She locked her arms around his neck and kissed the side of his throat. She could feel the wild jump of his pulse. The faintly salty tang of his skin seeped onto her tongue.

He carried her into the suite's elegantly furnished bedroom. Lucy glanced around wonderingly, absorbing a myriad of sensual details.

Flowers blossomed luxuriously out of a variety of vases. Roses, mostly. Brilliantly scarlet. Blush pink. Ivory pale. Her favorite copper-coral, too. There were arrangements of exotic-looking orchids and fragrant freesia, as well.

An iced bottle of champagne was nestled in a silver bucket that had been placed on a nightstand to the right of the bed. Two slender long-stemmed glasses sat next to the bucket. Lucy's vision blurred for a moment as she realized that the glasses were engraved. The letters *L* and *C* had been etched into the bubble-thin crystal, their curving lines intertwined like lovers.

"Oh, Ch-Chris..."

"Happy honeymoon, Lucy," the man she'd married said as she faltered on the verge of sentimental tears. "And happy New Year, as well."

The king-size bed's coverlet and blankets had been neatly turned back, revealing an inviting expanse of snowy-white linen. Bracing one knee against the edge of the mattress, Chris placed her down on the cool, crisp sheets. He then stroked his fingers though her hair, fanning it out against the pillowcase.

His movements were slow. Deliberate. Precise. As though he had all the time in the world at his command and intended to utilize every single second of it.

Lucy gazed up at her husband, mesmerized by his concentration and control. Lifting her left hand, she placed it gently against his right cheek. A gold band glinted on her ring finger, along with a flawless square-cut diamond, the precious symbol of the pledges she'd made less than seven hours ago in accordance with the word of God and the statutes of the state of Illinois.

Straightening, Chris kicked off his shoes. Then he stretched out on the bed and took her into his arms. She molded herself against him, tilting her face upward, wanting to feel his mouth on hers once again.

Their lips met. Fused. Their tongues teased and tantalized. The taste of him merged with the taste of her and became the honeyed essence of mutual desire.

Lucy moaned softly, moved sinuously. Experience had taught her some of the things that excited the man she loved. Instinct instructed her about most of the others. She let her hands roam up and down his back and torso, relishing the sleek ripple and release of well-toned muscle and sinew.

The catch on the front of her bra gave way to the coaxing of clever but not-quite-steady fingers. Cool air eddied briefly over freshly bared skin. Lucy shivered, catching her bottom lip between her teeth to mute a whimper of anticipation. A moment later, she felt the claiming cup of her husband's palms against her naked flesh. She closed her eyes, arching into the allurement of his caress.

"Beautiful," she heard Chris murmur in a reverent, rough-velvet voice. His hands were urgent, yet exquisitely gentle. He seemed to understand even better than she did where and how and when she wanted to be touched. "You're so beautiful."

And then she felt his mouth. His hot, hungry mouth, closing over the tip of her right breast. Licking. Laving. Sampling. Sucking. Each time his lips exerted their suctioning pressure on the burgeoning peak, there was an answering throb deep within her body.

Lucy opened her eyes. She uttered Chris's name on a shaky whisper, her fingers spasming against his shoulders. Her nails bit briefly into the taut flesh of his upper arms as he transferred his attentions to her left breast. Again he suckled, drawing her aching nipple deep into his mouth. Again she experienced the yearning clench of response in her womb.

Chris kissed a path upward from Lucy's bosom, drinking in the soft, swooning cry she made when his lips finally reclaimed hers. He was starving, he thought dizzily, and she was a feast to sate all his senses. But the more he tasted of her—the more he touched, smelled, heard and saw—the more acutely he hungered.

"Yes," she said on a sigh when he finally ended the kiss. "Oh, yes."

He undid her sheer stockings and carefully peeled them off. Lucy watched silently as he did so, her expression ratcheting up old appetites at the same time it roused new ones. Her cheeks were flushed, almost feverish-looking. Her ripe mouth was moist and trembling.

My wife, he told himself triumphantly, touching the ball of his thumb against the plain gold ring that now adorned his left hand. *My . . . wife.*

He charted the shape of her legs with his hands in ardent, appreciative stages. From her prettily pedicured toes to her well-turned ankles. From her well-turned ankles to the backs of her knees. From the backs of her knees to the satin-cream skin of her inner thighs.

His fingertips hovered for an instant at the apex of her limbs, brushing lightly against the dampened fabric that shielded the entrance to her feminine core. His mind flashed back to the first time they'd made love. To the crazy jumble of emotions he'd experienced knowing that he was to be the recipient of something that could be surrendered only once.

He'd felt awed.

He'd felt unworthy.

He'd felt invincible.

He felt much the same right now.

"Chris—" Lucy began in a half-suffocated voice, propping herself up on her elbows.

"I need you, sweetheart," he said huskily, sliding his palms over the silky fabric of her panties and hooking his thumbs beneath the lace-trimmed top edge. "All of you."

Her dark lashes fluttered down a fraction of an inch, veiling a wildfire kindling in the depths of her expressive eyes. The corners of her lips curled in the start of a smile that sizzled through his bloodstream. A throbbing heaviness invaded his loins. Desire clawed in his gut like a jungle cat.

A languid lift of lushly feminine hips.

A swift downward tug by long-fingered male hands.

The last scrap of Lucy's lingerie fluttered to the plushly carpeted floor, leaving her naked.

Chris swallowed convulsively, struggling for control as he surveyed the newly revealed flesh and the lovely triangle of dark, glossy curls. He disciplined himself to ease up, shift back. Forced himself to get to his feet.

He opened the buckle of his belt. Unzipped his fly.

Shucked his trousers and the briefs beneath them down his legs in a single seamless movement.

Kicked the garments off . . . and away.

Lucy's breath jammed in her throat at the sight of Chris's sleekly powerful physique and flagrantly aroused masculinity. She'd been afraid the first time, she dimly remembered. Not so much of the hurt, although she'd been warned that was inevitable. No, her deepest fear had centered around the awful possibility that she'd fail to please at something it seemed all her friends found as natural as scratching.

There had been no hurt. A moment of discomfort, yes, but one so buffered by tenderness that she could scarcely be sure she'd really experienced it. And if she'd been less than adequate in her innocence, she hadn't been able to discern it. Chris had responded to her as though she were Eve incarnate.

She dragged her gaze slowly upward, conscious of the pound-pound-pounding of her blood. She could hear it, hammering in her ears. She could feel it, pulsing in the tips of her toes and fingers.

Dark eyes locked with hazel ones, much as they'd done on a hot summer night barely six months before.

Lucy lifted her arms.

Chris rejoined her on the king-size bed.

They kissed. Caressed. Rolled across the crisp white sheets in a tangle of perspiration-sheened legs and arms. She found herself laughing with joy one moment, gasping in shocked pleasure the next. She said her husband's name over and over again. He murmured hers, and a dozen different endearments besides. Then, in a lightning-quick change of mood, he nipped at the lobe of her right ear and began whispering a litany of darkly delicious promises.

His hands were everywhere. Testing. Tempting. Torching her flesh. She reciprocated in kind, charting the strong expanse of his shoulders, the long, taut line of his torso and the flat plane of his stomach. The shallow indentation of his navel held her strangely in thrall for several shuddering seconds, and then she shifted her tactile attentions downward a few inches.

"Lucy." Chris speared his fingers through her hair. "Oh . . . Lucy."

"Yes." The word was an affirmation. An invitation. *"Yes."*

They rolled over again. She ended up beneath him, feeling the nudge of his knee between her thighs as his mouth took hers in another searing kiss.

She opened eagerly, arching upward in welcome as Chris filled her with a strong, sure thrust. A glorious sensation surged through her veins. She wrapped her arms and legs around him as her consciousness narrowed to exclude everything but the moment . . . and the man.

Chris groaned hoarsely, his embrace tightening. His spine bowed, the intimacy of his possession of her increasing by a few ineffably exquisite degrees.

Closer. And closer still.

She shuddered, her body convulsing on the brink of sensory overload. Her brain seemed to blank out, as though it were too overwhelmed to form anything approaching a coherent thought. Then, suddenly, she shattered.

An instant later, she felt her partner do the same.

Lucy had wondered if it would be different, making love as husband and wife, not simply man and woman. In the midst of a molten flood of ecstasy, she learned that it was. Deeply, indescribably different.

She'd never dreamed that it could be better.

She should have.

Chris liked to cuddle afterward.

This had taken Lucy by surprise. According to her female friends, most guys were savvy enough to understand that most girls expected some foreplay before the main event. Unfortunately, these friends averred, disappointingly few members of the opposite sex had gotten it through their thick skulls that women craved a little *after*play, too.

"They get off," Tina Roberts had once informed her with a disdainful gesture. "They want you to tell 'em it was great.

They roll over and start snoring. And if they don't sack out right away, they reach for a cigarette or the TV remote control. Then they tell you to bring 'em a beer. Or make 'em a sandwich. You want to prolong the mood? *Forget about it.* You know that joke about the guy who says his ideal girl is one who'll put out, then turn into a sausage pizza? Well, I'm not laughing.''

"So, Mrs. Banks," Chris murmured, brushing Lucy's forehead with his lips. His hand skimmed lightly over her hip, triggering an echo of breath-stealing bliss.

Lucy snuggled close, planting a kiss on the ridge of his collarbone as she savored the strength of his encircling arms. She could feel the steady drumbeat of his heart. My husband, she thought proudly. This is my husband.

"So, Mr. Banks," she returned after a few moments, relishing the words.

"How do you feel?"

A giggle tickled at the back of her throat. She released it, then replied, "Married."

"Me, too." Chris chuckled deep in his chest. The sound rumbled against her ear, stirring nerves that had just begun to settle.

"Do you like it?"

He turned his head slightly, a lock of light brown hair falling forward onto his brow. His gaze met hers. "More than I can say."

They kissed. Slowly. Sweetly.

They kissed again. Still slowly. Still sweetly. But with a lick of heat beneath the sugar.

"Would *madame* care for a little liquid refreshment?" Chris eventually inquired. His skin was flushed, his voice a note or two lower than it had been the last time he spoke.

Lucy moistened her lips, enjoying the glinting response she saw in the depths of his hazel eyes. "Very much."

He sat up, seemingly at ease with his nudity. She watched him pluck the champagne bottle from the silver bucket, then strip off the foil and undo the restraining twists of wire. He performed the movements with deft efficiency.

As he reached for the engraved crystal flutes, she levered herself up beside him. She saw one corner of his mobile mouth quirk as she draped the sheet around her. She supposed it *was* a bit late for modesty, given her wanton, wedded behavior of just a short time before. Still . . .

"Chilly?" Chris teased, handing her the glasses.

"Not at the moment." Her response was demure.

"Well, let me know if the situation changes."

"And if it does?"

"Then I'll find a way—" the cork succumbed to the pressure of his thumbs with a soft pop "—to get you warm again."

Lucy extended the flutes. Forget warm, she thought, her fingers tightening on the fragile crystal stems. She was already feeling *hot*.

The wine poured out in a frothy stream, bubbles dancing in its pale depths like pinpoint jewels. Ice cubes clinked as Chris set the bottle back in the silver bucket. She gave him one of the glasses she was holding, her fingertips brushing his as they completed the handoff. The brief contact sent an electric tingle arrowing up her arm.

"To us?" he proposed huskily, his eyes steady on hers.

"To us," she concurred.

They toasted and drank deeply. The sparkling wine danced down Lucy's throat like liquid sunshine. It was the most delicious thing she'd ever tasted.

"I think we should make a resolution," she announced boldly when she lowered her glass. She'd never known such a sense of completeness.

"A resolution?"

"To live happily ever after."

Chris smiled in a fashion that made her head start to spin. Her bloodstream seemed to be fizzing. "Together."

"Abso—" she hiccuped "—lutely."

Lucia Annette Banks—nee Falco—and Christopher Dodson Banks went their separate ways less than twelve months later.

One

"It's not right, Lucy," Tiffany Tarrington Toulouse declared, a combination of frustration and concern muting the usual sparkle in her pale gray eyes. "A lovely girl like you, spending New Year's Eve alone. You did the same thing last year. And the year before that."

Lucy Falco suppressed a sigh. She'd never told her colleagues at Gulliver's Travels that the holiday under discussion had very bittersweet associations for her. Although nearly everyone in the office was vaguely aware that she'd gone through a divorce about a decade ago, she'd avoided offering any concrete details about her marriage or the bustup that had followed.

There were two main reasons for this. Her position as office manager of the Atlanta-based travel agency was one of them. As much as she genuinely liked the men and women she supervised, she felt a managerial responsibility to keep her private life separate from her professional one. That this "responsibility" was at odds with her penchant for getting involved in other people's personal problems was something of which she was well aware. But there it was.

The second reason she shied away from explaining why her marriage had ended was that she was no longer sure she knew. What she once would have cited as incontrovertible fact—that Chris had been the unmitigated wronger and she the blameless wrongee—now seemed to her to be open to at least some degree of argument.

Which wasn't to say that she regretted her divorce. She didn't. Not...really. Given the life she'd built for herself in the wake of it, how could she? The woman she was today was pretty much the one she'd aspired to be before the sweltering summer night Christopher Dodson Banks walked into Falco's Pizzeria and turned her world upside down.

Would she have become this woman if she'd stayed married? A decade ago, Lucia Annette Falco would have said absolutely not. But lately, she'd begun to wonder.

A decade ago, she also would have maintained that her marriage had been unsalvageable. She'd begun to wonder about the validity of *that* assessment with increasing frequency in recent times, too.

"There's always a lot of end-of-the-year business to be taken care of, Tiff," Lucy said, dropping her gaze and making a show of shuffling through the files on the top of her antique burled-cherry desk. "I have a huge backlog of paperwork to wade through."

"If there's so much to be done, why did you give everyone the rest of the week off?" the older woman asked challengingly, fluffing her frothy mane of silvery white curls with an extravagantly beringed hand.

"Because I felt like it."

This deliberately outrageous explanation stopped Tiffany for a moment. But only a moment. She rose from the tall wingback chair in which she'd been ensconced. *"Lucia Annette Falco—"*

"I appreciate your concern," Lucy told her, meaning it. "But not having plans to party hearty on New Year's Eve doesn't mean I'm socially deprived. I'm simply not into swilling champagne and kissing strangers at the stroke of midnight."

Tiffany arched a well-plucked brow and pursed her plum-glossed lips. Then, with a sassiness that belied her sixty-plus years, she retorted, "Don't knock it unless you've tried it."

Lucy had to laugh.

Clearly sensing an opening, the older woman reverted to her initial theme. It was a characteristic response. For all her flamboyant flutterings, Tiffany was an expert at manipulating other people for what she considered to be their own good. She was also as tenacious as a lockjawed terrier when she got her teeth into something. It was little wonder that she was one of Gulliver's Travels' most successful agents.

"You don't have to stay out all night," she coaxed. "But what'd be the harm in dashing home and putting on something extra-pretty, then meeting Hastings and me for a teensy-weensy libation at the Buckhead Ritz?"

"Oh, I'm sure Hastings would just love to have me horn in on your big date," Lucy riposted. Hastings Chatwell Lee IV, as she and everyone else at the agency was aware, was Tiffany's latest beau.

"He'd rather have me all to himself, of course." The response was smug. Tiffany Tarrington Toulouse was a woman who was gloriously sure of the irresistibility of her feminine charms. "But if it'd make me happy to have you come along..."

There was no need for her to finish the sentence. From what Lucy had observed, Hastings Chatwell Lee IV would lie down like a rug and let himself be stomped on by a herd of hobnail-booted hippos if he had an inkling that it would please his silver-haired sweetie pie.

"It's a tempting offer, Tiff," she acknowledged after a few seconds. "But I'm going to pass."

A hint of steel entered Tiffany's eyes. She opened her mouth, plainly intending to press her case. She was forestalled by the precipitous arrival of a gangly young man whose buzz-cut platinum hair and small silver nose ring were in striking contrast to his starched white shirt—complete with pocket protector—crisply ironed khaki pants and spit-polished penny loafers.

The young man's name was Wayne Dweck, and he'd recently joined Gulliver's Travels as a part-time office assistant. Wayne was passionately interested in computer technology and so-called alternative music. It was Lucy's impression that he spent the bulk of his free time alternating between surfing the Internet and slam-dancing.

"'Scuse me, Ms. Toulouse," he said, a bit breathlessly. "But you've got a seriously expensive long-distance phone call. Some guy named Sergei, from St. Petersburg."

"Sergei from St. Petersburg?" Lucy lifted her brows inquiringly.

"Sergei Illyanovich Gennady," Tiffany elaborated with an airy gesture. "I met him last summer, on that singles cruise I took. You remember. The one to the Galapagos Islands. Such a nice man. It's hard to believe he was a godless Communist for most of his life. He's probably calling to wish me happy New Year." She turned a beaming smile on Wayne and patted him on the cheek, her rings glinting. "Thank you, dear."

The nostril-pierced part-timer turned beet red, his Adam's apple bobbing up and down like a Ping-Pong ball on a choppy sea. "N-no problem, Ms. Toulouse. My p-pleasure."

Tiffany returned her crystalline gaze to Lucy. "You think about what I said," she instructed firmly, then pivoted on her heel and walked away. There was a hint of Mae West in the sway of her hips.

"She is so...*totally*... cool," Wayne declared in an ardently admiring tone, sagging briefly against the door frame.

"She's totally something, all right," Lucy wryly agreed.

"She should have her own home page on the Web." The gawky office assistant ambled forward and plunked himself down in the chair Tiffany had vacated a short time before. "Do you think she'd mind if I started one? I could call it Travels with Tiffany, and I could post pictures from all the trips she's taken. Maybe get her to write some commentary. I could link it to some of the other outstanding babe sites, too."

Lucy bit the inside of her cheek, struggling to keep a straight face. "I think Tiffany would probably be flattered by the idea. Why don't you talk to her about it first thing next week?"

It was difficult to believe that Wayne could blush more vividly than he had a minute or so earlier, but he managed it.

"You mean, like, face-to-face?" he gasped, gripping the arms of the wingback chair. "On a ... reality ... basis?"

"Mmm-hmm ..."

There was an uncomfortable pause. After much squirming, Wayne finally said, "Maybe ... Maybe I'll E-mail her about it. I kind of have trouble keeping my head straight when she's there in the, uh, flesh, you know? I get sort of warm and woozy. The first time I was introduced to her, it was right after I'd had lunch at that Mexican place over on Spring and I was scared I was going to blow burrito chunks in front of her. I've pretty much got that under control now, though. Not the warm and woozy part. The potential hurling."

"I'm glad to hear it."

"The thing is, I think Ms. Toulouse in one of those women who was born with megapheromones."

"Excuse me?"

"Pheromones. Like, sex chemicals. Bugs secrete them, big-time."

"Oh."

"It has to do with smell, mostly. Human pheromones, that is. I mean, sometimes you sniff somebody, and *wham*. Instant attraction." Wayne cocked his head, his brow furrowing. "Did that ever happen to you, Lucy?"

Her pulse stuttered. Memory assailed her, sending a ripple of heat coursing through her body.

The subtle appeal of expensive spice.

The more provocative allure of natural male musk.

Chris's scent.

Oh, yes. Lucia Annette Falco knew what it was like to "sniff" a stranger and plunge headlong into love. Or lust. Or some irresistible blending of the two. And although it had been nearly ten years since—

"Lucy?"

She started, more than a little appalled at the waywardly erotic direction of her thoughts. She'd come to expect a certain amount of nostalgic weirdness from herself on New Year's Eve. But this was ridiculous! It was even worse than the eager way she'd devoured that newspaper profile of Chris she happened to run across a few weeks back.

"I'm sorry, Wayne," she said, shutting her mind to the memory of the distinguished-looking black-and-white photograph that had accompanied the laudatory article. "Yes. It happened to me. I once . . . sniffed . . . a man and was attracted to him. But it was a long, long time ago."

"Well, I wasn't trying to be nosy. . . ." Wayne stopped, frowning. Then he started to snicker. "Nosy," he repeated. "About whether you ever got turned on by smelling some guy." The snickering became snorting laughter. "Heh-heh-heh. *Nosy.* I like that."

Lucy didn't, for a variety of reasons. She gave the young man a few seconds to recover from his self-induced amusement, then reclaimed control of the conversation. "Shifting to a more serious subject, Wayne," she began, in her crispest executive voice. "What's the status on the new software?"

The younger man blinked several times, clearly lost. "The new software?"

"That Mr. Gulliver ordered."

"Oh, yeah. Of course." Wayne grinned broadly, back in the loop. "It's cool. Cutting-edge, but easy to upgrade. Mr.

G. really knows his stuff. I was just finishing installing it when that Sergei guy called for Ms. Toulouse."

"Good work." Lucy was a firm believer in positive reinforcement.

"Thanks. I'm gonna wait a couple of weeks before I start programming the specialty functions. 'Cause, like, I figure people need time to get used to the basic system before they can decide what kind of shortcuts they want."

"That sounds sensible."

"Just one thing." Wayne's expression became wheedling, underscoring his youth. "Are you *sure* you don't want me to load the encryption system I showed you last week? I've been using it at my workstation since Christmas. It's awesome, Lucy."

"I'm sure it is." So awesome, she didn't have a clue about how it worked or why the agency would want to utilize it. About the only thing she remembered from the enthusiastic demonstration Wayne had given her was the sequence of keystrokes that supposedly enabled him to send coded E-mail anywhere in the world.

"Well, then—"

"We're not the Pentagon, Wayne."

"Jeez, I hope not! Do you have any idea how easy it is to access most of the Defense Department's data banks?"

Lucy stiffened, flashing on a scenario in which Gulliver's Travels was invaded by federal agents and shut down as a hotbed of hacker activity.

"Oh, hey..." the young man forged on, apparently oblivious of the alarm his previous—and pray God, rhetorical—query had triggered. "Speaking of security and breaking into things. You know how we've been wondering what they've been storing in the vault next door? Well, a friend of a friend of a friend of mine knows this guy who's related to somebody in the police department, and he says he heard—"

"*Wayne!*"

The source of this urgent exclamation was Jim Burns, another one of Gulliver's Travels' top agents. He was short, superenergized and given to wearing plaid shirts with polka-dot ties. His rather checkered résumé included stints as a short-order cook and a used-car salesman.

"Jimmy?" Lucy questioned, instantly concerned. The last time she'd seen her co-worker looking so distressed had been the day he discovered that the cruise package he'd put together as the grand prize for a local Halloween charity ball had landed the couple who'd won it in the middle of a modern-day pirate drama. The aftermath of the episode—the capture and prosecution of the members of a drug-smuggling operation—had been front-page news. Fortunately, Gulliver's Travels had suffered no negative PR fall-out. Not only that, the couple who had gotten caught up in the adventure had already booked another trip through the agency. "What's wrong?"

"I'm being overrun by aliens from a parallel universe!"

She gawked. *Aliens from a parallel universe?*

"Did you try the death beam?" Wayne asked calmly, unfolding his lanky frame and getting to his feet.

"Nonfunctional." Jimmy pulled out a handkerchief and blotted his perspiration-sheened brow. "Even worse, I forfeited my powers of transmogrification when I cut a deal with the Fungocians on level three."

"You cut a deal with the *Fungocians?*" The office assistant was visibly startled. Even his nose ring seemed to quiver with disbelief. "Jeez, Jimmy. They're the scum of the universe!"

"I thought I could double-cross them before they double-crossed me."

"Never going to happen, dude." Wayne glanced at Lucy. "'Scuse me. I gotta go kick some alien butt."

"Have fun," she answered ironically.

Jimmy lingered in the doorway after the younger man exited. "Sorry about that, Lucy."

She brushed the apology aside, not really upset at having had her conversation with Wayne interrupted. "Another computer game?" she asked knowingly.

"A Christmas gift from the kids."

"Ah."

The agent shifted his weight from one foot to the other. "I was only fiddling with it because things have been really slow."

"No need to explain, Jimmy." And there wasn't. Jim Burns had his share of eccentricities. But when it came down to the crunch, Lucy knew he could be counted on to deliver for the agency. If he wanted to spend his spare moments fighting aliens from a parallel universe, she had no objections. "I know how quiet it's been. I'm about ready to tell everyone to pack it in till next year."

"Give us a jump on celebrating the auld lang syne, eh?"

"Something like that."

"Everybody's really excited about having the rest of the week off, you know."

"It's no more than you deserve. The agency had a terrific fourth quarter. Mr. Gulliver is going to be very pleased."

"Have you heard from him lately?"

"Not since I got that fax requesting all those honeymoon brochures."

"He actually got hitched on Christmas Eve, huh?"

"So I gather."

"I'll bet there's quite a story behind that marriage."

"Probably." Lucy kept her voice noncommittal. What inside information she had about their elusive boss's sudden plunge into matrimonial waters, she didn't intend to share. Nor was she about to mention her unwitting but undeniably crucial role in the affair. "I don't think we should go digging around trying to find out what it is, though."

"Butt into Mr. Gulliver's personal life?" Jimmy shook his head in unequivocal rejection. "No way. Nosiree. What he wants me to know, he'll tell me. What he wants to keep private, I'm gonna keep my nose out of." He paused, his expression turning thoughtful. "It kind of creeped me out in the beginning, you know. Mr. Gulliver's only communicating with us through faxes, E-mail and over the phone, that is. And it was always business, business, business with him. But I started sensing a change of tone right after Thanksgiving. Well, no. A little before that, actually. I mean, even though you said you'd square it away with him, I expected to get fired once he found out about my booking Josh and Cari Keegan on a cruise that turned out to be a front for drug runners! But the boss was really understanding about it. And then he personally picked up the tab for the agency's Christmas open house—"

"The First Annual, Fabulously Famous Gulliver's Travels Holiday Party, you mean," Lucy corrected, invoking the grandiose title by which the bash was known around the office.

"Yeah. Right." Jimmy grinned reminiscently. "That was some blowout, huh?"

"That it was."

"Think the boss might spring for another shindig around Mardi Gras?"

"*Jimmy!*"

"Just kidding. Although it *would* be a good way to recycle those masks Tiffany bought for that big New Orleans promotion we did about eighteen months back."

"I can definitely picture you wearing the one with the purple plumes," she retorted with a quick laugh.

"Nah. I've got my eye on the alligator headpiece." He winked. "Speaking of holiday shindigs—what kind of plans do you have for tonight?"

The query caught Lucy off guard, although it probably shouldn't have. She managed a casual shrug and reverted to the paper-shuffling ploy she'd used with Tiffany. "Oh, this and that."

"Meaning you're going to stay home by yourself. Just like last year. And the year before that."

She looked up. She did not want to go through this again. "You think there's something wrong with that?"

"No. Of course not. I mean, you have mixed feelings about the holiday, right? I can understand that."

Lucy's heart seemed to skip a beat. "You . . . can?"

"Sure. For all the hoopla, New Year's Eve is really a time for taking stock. And that can be a little depressing. You find yourself looking back on all the things you *intended* to get done in the previous three-hundred-sixty-odd days and realizing that you never got around to doing any of 'em. Then you feel compelled to make a bunch of resolutions that you know deep down you're never going to—"

"I don't do that."

The ex–used car salesman eyed her curiously for a few moments, plainly taken aback by the sharpness of her assertion. Lucy shifted uneasily, wishing she'd kept quiet.

"You don't?" he finally asked.

An echo reached Lucy across the distance of eleven years. Words from her wedding night. Words that were etched in her brain. Imprinted on her heart.

I think we should make a resolution.

A resolution?

To live happily ever after.

Together?

Absolutely.

"Not...anymore," she clarified, tempering her tone and disciplining her features to hide the pain she was feeling. No matter that the passage of time was supposed to heal all wounds. It still hurt to remember how she and Chris had toasted the resolution she'd proposed. How they'd pledged their mutual love with words and deeds.

They'd made a beautiful, beautiful beginning together. But where had they ended up, a little more than twelve months later? In divorce court, citing irreconcilable differences!

"Yeah, well, I can understand that, too." Jimmy gave a little chuckle. "I've got this photocopied list I haul out once a year and read over. I've had it—gosh, I don't know—a decade, easy. It's the usual stuff. Lose weight. Get more exercise. Start putting money away for retirement."

Lucy forced a smile. "Those are all good things to resolve."

"Must be, considering I keep resolving 'em over and over." Another chuckle. "Anyway. If you *really* want to spend tonight all by your lonesome, that's your privilege. But I'm taking the family downtown to watch the Big Peach drop at midnight, and if you'd like to come along—"

"Thanks for the offer, but I'm really looking forward to having a quiet evening in."

"Are you sure? You're more than welcome to join us."

"I'm positive."

Jimmy hesitated, seeming to debate whether to shift into his pitchman mode. "Okay," he finally said, apparently persuaded by something in her expression that this was one sale he wasn't going to make. "It's your call. I, uh, guess I'll go check on how Wayne's doing with aliens."

"Don't make any more bargains with the Fuzzie-whatsises."

"The Fungocians. And I won't."

"See you next year, Jimmy."

"Count on it, Lucy."

Two

Chris Banks sat on the edge of the king-size bed in his hotel suite, staring at the telephone. He was contemplating what he knew was either the second-best or the second-worst idea he'd ever had in his life, and the circumstances that had brought him to the point of acting upon it.

Do it, Banks, he told himself. Just . . . *do* it.

He reached for the receiver.

Picked it up.

Pressed nine to get an outside line.

Then, meticulously, he punched out the seven-digit telephone number that he'd gotten from directory assistance less than a week ago.

One ring.

He hadn't known where his ex-wife was living when he began exploring the possibility of becoming the executive legal counsel for an Atlanta-based philanthropic foundation. He'd picked up that information during a wholly unplanned—and not particularly pleasant—pre-Christmas encounter with Lucy's former maid of honor, Tina Roberts.

It had happened at the perfume counter of one of Chicago's biggest department stores. He'd been doing some last-minute holiday shopping.

"Can I help you?" a nasal female voice had inquired.

"I hope so," he'd answered wryly, looking up from the mind-boggling display of fragrances he'd been examining. He'd felt a jolt of recognition as he focused on the saleswoman who'd addressed him. "Tina?" he'd blurted out. "Tina...Roberts?"

The woman had stared at him. She hadn't spoken.

It *was* Tina, he'd thought. She'd been about fifty pounds heavier and considerably blonder than the last time he saw her, but it was definitely she.

"You...probably don't remember me," he'd said after a few awkward seconds, debating whether to extend his hand. Something in Tina's artfully lined eyes had warned him that it would more likely be snapped off than shaken. He'd opted for self-preservation over politesse and kept his hand by his side. "It's been quite a while. I'm Christopher Banks. I used to be married to—"

Two rings.

"I know who you are." The response had been curt. "And my name's Tina Palucci now. What are you doing here? I heard you lived in New York."

"I do." He'd been startled by the fact that someone from Lucy's neighborhood circle had apparently been keeping tabs on his whereabouts. He'd left Chicago for a clerkship in Washington shortly after his divorce was finalized. He'd then moved on to the partnership track of a well-known law firm in Manhattan. "I'm back visiting my family for a few days."

"Oh. Right. Your *family.*"

His gut had tightened at the way she inflected the final word. Good sense had dictated that he terminate the conversation as quickly as possible. But he hadn't been able to.

Compelled by a combination of emotions too jumbled to sort out, he'd asked, "Have you seen...Lucy...recently?"

Tina had given him a scathing look, apparently deeming him unworthy to utter his ex-wife's name. He hadn't been inclined to challenge whether her hostility was justified.

"Lucy's in Atlanta," she'd said.

"Atlanta?" He'd been stunned to the point of stupidity by the coincidence. "G-Georgia?"

"Whaddya think? Atlanta, Wyoming?"

"You mean, she—she lives there?"

"That right. She's the office manager of an agency called Gulliver's Travels." Tina had used the words like a gauntlet, clearly relishing the opportunity to smack him across the face with some salient facts about his ex-wife. "It's a great job. She's made a terrific life for herself. Lucy's *very* successful."

"I'm glad to hear it." And he had been. "I always expected that she would be."

Three rings.

Chris forked his free hand through his hair. The foundation had flown him to Atlanta for a final round of interviews yesterday. A firm offer had been made over breakfast this morning. He'd promised a firm answer within a week.

He'd intended to head back to Manhattan to mull his future. Mother Nature had had other plans. When he checked in for his return flight at Hartsfield International Airport, he'd been told that there'd be a departure delay because of weather conditions in the New York metropolitan area. About an hour later, his flight and scores of others had been cancelled.

Having less than no desire to spend New Year's Eve camped out at the airport, he'd gotten on the telephone and started calling hotels. The first seven places had been booked solid by holiday revellers. The clerk at the eighth had perkily announced that there'd been a last-minute cancelation and she could offer him a suite. He'd snapped it up without asking the price, reeling off his credit-card number to guarantee the reservation. He'd then grabbed a cab and gone back into Atlanta.

So here he was, stuck in the city his ex-wife now called home, on what would have been their tenth wedding anniversary had he not behaved like a—

Four rings.

Pickup, followed by a whisper of static.

And then, a mellifluous female voice. It was a voice that Christopher Dodson Banks hadn't heard for nearly a decade.

Except in his dreams.

"Hi, there," the voice said, sending a tremor of response racing through his body. "You've reached 555-3827 and this is Lucy Falco's answering machine. Unlike some of my kind, I have faith in humanity. I truly believe you're going to do the right thing and leave your name, number and a brief message after the beep. But just in case you're contemplating some other course of action, please be advised that I'm equipped with caller ID. This means that I have your number stored in my data bank and can track you down if you hang up on me. So be smart. Live up to my high opinion of you and leave a message." *Beep!*

Chris's heart was hammering against his ribs. He opened his mouth to speak.

Nothing came out.

After several seconds he closed his mouth. Then he replaced the phone in its cradle. His hands were shaking.

"Damn," he whispered. "Dammit to hell."

Chris sat motionless for nearly a minute. Finally he reached for his suit jacket, which he'd taken off earlier and laid beside him on the bed. He extracted a slim leatherbound appointment book and began thumbing through it. He was stalling, and he knew it. There was no need for him to look up the address of the business establishment he had in mind. Like Lucy's home telephone number, he could recite it by heart.

Gulliver's Travels. 2511 Peachtree—

Chris slapped the appointment book shut and glanced at his wristwatch. It was a few minutes before five.

Just about closing time, he reflected with a grimace. Maybe even past it, given that this was New Year's Eve. Chances were, Lucy was long gone from her office. Chances were, she was out of the business mode and into the social groove.

He could imagine her, primping for a night on the town. Although she hadn't devoted a lot of time to fussing with her appearance while they were together, there had been a couple of occasions during their short marriage when she pulled out all the stops.

Having never lived with a woman, he'd found himself utterly fascinated by Lucy's grooming rituals. He'd been turned on by them, too, if truth be told. And as for what he'd felt when he got a gander at the finished product...

Chris clenched his hands. Despite his best efforts to block them, his mind's eye filled with a series of images.

Lucy.

Brushing her long dark hair with slow, sexy strokes, then pinning it up in a style that just begged to be taken down.

Lucy.

Slipping on her lacy lingerie piece by provocative piece, offering a blood-heating preview of what would be waiting *after* the public partying.

Lucy—

Doing those things and more for another man.

Christopher Dodson Banks cursed under his breath, clamping down on a surge of jealousy he knew he had no right to feel. He'd had his chance, and he'd screwed it up.

He'd fallen head over heels in love with Lucia Annette Falco eleven and a half years ago. But as deeply as he cared for her, he'd lacked the insight—the sensitivity—to fully understand what kind of person she was and how she viewed the world. His failure to comprehend these fundamental truths had led him to commit an act of betrayal that precipitated the end of his marriage.

He checked his watch again. It was now five after five.

Gulliver's Travels was an inexpensive cab ride away. He knew this because he'd mentioned its address to the hotel's concierge and inquired about its proximity after he checked in. The concierge had consulted a small directory, then informed him that the location in question fell within something called the "convention zone."

"It's a flat fare if you take a taxi from this hotel," the man had explained. "Quick trip. Very reasonable. You could walk it in, oh, twenty minutes on a nice day. But on a cold night like this..."

"I'm from New York," Chris had returned. "Anything above zero is balmy to me."

The concierge had smiled sympathetically. "I understand, sir. Still, we don't recommend that our guests go out walking by themselves after dark."

He had Lucy's agency's telephone number, Chris reminded himself. He could always call.

And then what?

Another hang-up? Or maybe an impersonal request that Ms. Falco contact Mr. Banks at her earliest possible convenience?

No, he decided. He needed to do this—whatever "this" was going to turn out to be—face-to-face.

He'd take the flat-fare taxi ride to the office where Lucy evidently had earned the professional success he knew she'd grown up dreaming about achieving. If the place was closed for the holiday, so be it. At least he'd know exactly where it was and what it looked like. If it was still open and his ex-wife was there...

He had to see her again.

It was that simple.

And that complicated.

He was poised on the threshold of a new year, a word away from embarking on a new job in a new city. What better time to try to atone for old mistakes?

* * *

Lucy hung up the phone with a sigh. Bad enough that she'd had to finesse her colleagues' questions about her lack of holiday plans. Now her father and brothers—who, unlike her co-workers, were well aware of the reasons for her extremely ambivalent feelings about New Year's Eve—had taken to haranguing her about the situation, too.

"You don't have anybody to be with, you should come home," her father had insisted in a call that came in shortly after she told the rest of the agency's staff they could leave.

"I could be with somebody if I wanted to, Pop," she'd countered through gritted teeth, deciding to sidestep the coming-home issue entirely. Although she'd moved to Atlanta more than three years ago, her father refused to acknowledge that she actually lived there. He regarded the town house she'd bought as a temporary address. A sort of residential aberration. "But I don't."

"Why not? You still carrying a torch for that ex-husband of yours?"

"No!" It was not an original notion. Her brothers had started hinting at the possibility shortly after she passed the big three-oh with no sign of a serious suitor lurking on the horizon. Several of her uncles and cousins had taken to alluding to it, as well. But this was the first time anyone had had the nerve to broach the subject head-on. "Of course not!"

"Good. Because after what he did to you—"

"Pop, I'm sorry." She'd suddenly reached the end of her tether. She'd opted for an escape excuse that had proven effective in the past. "I've got a call coming in on the agency's priority line. It's probably my boss. Or a client with an international emergency. I have to go. Thanks for calling. Happy New Year. I'll talk with you soon."

Her eldest brother, Vinnie, had phoned five minutes later.

"Pop says you hung up on him, Lucy."

"I didn't hang up on him." She'd soothed herself with an assurance that this was technically true. Hanging up on someone meant slamming down the receiver without saying goodbye. "There was a phone call I had to take. Urgent agency business."

"Same kind of urgent agency business that came up the last two times I tried to talk to you?"

"Uh—"

"I hear you been usin' the 'I got urgent agency business' line on Joey and Mikey, too. And some of the uncles. Even when they call you at home."

Lucy had grimaced, realizing that she was going to have to come up with a new tactic for terminating conversations with her family. "I have a very demanding job. It's important to me."

"More important than your family bein' worried about you?"

"I've told you before. There is no—repeat, *no,* that's *n-o*—reason for anyone to be worried about me. I'm doing fine."

"Right now, maybe. But when I think about the way you looked the night you walked out on that bastard Banks—"

"That was more than ten years ago, Vinnie!"

"So? You think the people who really love you are ever gonna forget the expression on your face? You think they're ever gonna forget the sound of you cryin' like you'd never stop?"

Lucy massaged her temples, her brother's long-distance challenge echoing in her ears. She didn't expect him to understand. She didn't expect *anybody* to understand. How could she, given the tenuousness of her own grasp of what had happened and why?

She'd made a lot of mistakes on the night in question. Turning tail and retreating into the protective custody of her family had been the worst.

There was an awful irony about what she'd done. She'd expended a great deal of time and energy trying to persuade her many male relatives that she was more than capable of standing up for herself in what they universally agreed was a man's world. But when push came to shove, she'd behaved as though her spine were made of over-cooked linguini.

For the first time in her life, she'd acted like a victim. Like a helpless, hapless female.

And she'd been paying for it ever since.

Lucy glanced at her watch. It was nearly half past five. Time for her to be off. She rose to her feet and began gathering up her things. Her purse. Her coat. Her scarf. The files she needed to—

The telephone on her desk started to ring. Every instinct Lucy had warned her that the individual on the other end of the line was one of her brothers. Or maybe one of her uncles, depending on how efficient the Falco grapevine was on this particular evening.

She hesitated for a moment, then made up her mind. "I love you, guys," she said to the still-ringing phone. "But I'll talk to you next year."

She dashed out before she had a chance to relent.

Gulliver's Travels was located in a small four-story building with a central lobby. The guard behind the security desk—a skinny guy with a mustache—leaped to his feet as she came around the corner, heading toward the main exit.

"Wh-what are you d-doing here?" he demanded, his eyes darting back and forth. His mouth twitched, the hair on his upper lip wiggling like a mangy caterpillar.

"I work here."

"You . . . do?"

"I'm Lucy Falco. I'm office manager for Gulliver's Travels." She pointed in the direction from which she'd just come.

"Gulliver's T-Travels?" The guy gulped, paling a bit. "I thought everyone from there was g-gone by now!"

"I'm the last one out." Lucy frowned. She'd never encountered a security guard who seemed quite so...insecure. The man she was accustomed to seeing behind the desk when she left in the evening was an overweight ex-cop who was about as excitable as a box of rocks. "Where's Ray?"

"Ray?"

"Ray Price. The regular night watchman."

"Oh. *Him*. Well, uh, Ray's off." The man made a jerky gesture. "Because of the holiday. He's got seniority."

"I see." It made sense, Lucy decided after a moment's reflection. Ray had to be pushing sixty-five. "And you're—?"

"Here. Tonight. And tomorrow. Subbing for, uh, Ray."

"I meant your name."

"My name?" The guard's eyes widened. His lips twitched again. "Oh. Right. My name. It's, uh, T-Tom." He lifted a hand and tugged at the collar of his mud-brown uniform. "I'm just starting out at this, you know? Guarding, I mean. I'm a little . . . tense."

Inchoate suspicions gave way to compassionate understanding. Lucy could empathize with new-on-the-job nerves. She'd been tied up in knots during her first month at Gulliver's Travels.

"Just take a few deep breaths," she advised with a smile. "I'm sure everything will be just fine."

The mustachioed guard gave an odd little laugh. "I certainly hope so."

At that moment, the main door to the building swung open, admitting a blast of chilly wind and two equipment-laden men. The men—one bearded and bulky, one a balding bantamweight, both clad in midnight-blue jumpsuits—stopped dead in their tracks when they spotted Lucy.

There was a peculiar pause.

"Is there a problem, gentlemen?" Lucy finally felt compelled to ask.

The balding repairman cleared his throat then said, "Toilets, ma'am."

"*Toilets?*"

"Uh-huh," the bearded repairman affirmed, flashing a gap-toothed smile. "Toilets."

Lucy glanced at Tom. "There's trouble with the toilets?"

"S-some of 'em, yeah," he replied, fingering his collar again. "On the, uh, third floor."

"Overflow potential," the balding repairman stated. "Could get ugly."

Lucy wrinkled her nose distastefully at the image this statement conjured up. "Not exactly the nicest way to see out the old year."

The balding repairman shrugged, shifting his grip on the equipment he was holding. He didn't meet her eyes. "It'll be worth our while."

"Yeah." The bearded repairman bobbed his head and grinned happily, looking directly at her. "*Definitely* worth our while."

Remembering the outrageously high plumber's bill she'd had the previous winter, when two of her pipes had frozen and burst, Lucy didn't doubt this. That had been a "regular" job, and it had cost her what seemed like a small fortune. She couldn't imagine what the charge would be for work done after hours on a holiday!

"Well, better you than me," she said after a few moments. "I hope it doesn't take too long." Then she nodded at Tom. "Good night. Happy New Year."

"Uh, thanks. S-same to you."

Lucy headed for the heavy glass doors that opened onto the sidewalk, her heels clicking against the lobby's marble floor. She caught a glimpse of a bright yellow cab pulling up beside the curb. Although she normally rode mass transit to and from work, she occasionally treated herself to a taxi. Deciding to try to flag the vehicle down, she picked up her pace.

The godawful clatter of metal hitting polished stone made her check her step and pivot back toward the security desk, her heart thudding. The bearded repairman apparently had dropped his equipment.

"It's okay, ma'am!" the guard called loudly.

Lucy hesitated. "Are you sure?"

"Positive!" The guard waved her off. "Everything's under control!"

It didn't *look* under control, Lucy reflected, watching the two repairmen scrabble around on the floor. And Tom's voice sounded just a wee bit panicked.

Oh, well. It really wasn't her concern.

She turned and pushed one of the heavy glass doors open.

A split second after stepping out into the chill night air, she collided with someone. A pair of hands gripped her forearms, preventing her from toppling over. She caught a tantalizing whiff of spice and musk.

Lifting her gaze, Lucy found herself staring up into a leanly handsome face that she hadn't seen in the flesh for nearly a decade. Her vision seemed to blur. She began to feel the way Wayne Dweck had claimed he felt around Tiffany Tarrington Toulouse. Warm. Woozy. And vaguely in danger of losing her lunch.

"Ch-Chris?" she whispered, barely able to utter the name.

"Lucy." Her ex-husband sounded stunned. He looked the same way. "You . . . you cut your hair."

Three

On a scale of one to ten—with one representing the worst possible thing a man could say to his ex-wife upon encountering her for the first time in nearly a decade and ten representing the most suavely brilliant—Chris rated his opening gambit a 2.5.

Lucy's expression suggested that she'd mark his effort lower. A *lot* lower. Like, maybe—if she was feeling exceptionally generous—a minus three. Her verbal response underscored this impression.

"Yes," she snapped, jerking herself free of his grasp and glaring at him. "I cut my hair. Do you have a problem with that?"

"No. Of course not. It looks...nice." And it did. Where Lucy's hair had once tumbled to the middle of her back, it now skimmed her shoulders and feathered across her forehead. The style was sleekly sophisticated. It emphasized the dark beauty of her eyes and made her cheekbones seem more prominent. Or maybe that was makeup. While the illumination where they were standing wasn't the greatest, Chris had the impression that his ex-wife was doing more to her face than she had a decade ago. "It's just that...well, I've spent a lot of years visualizing you with long hair."

Lucy arched a brow in an achingly familiar fashion, clearly unmoved by his complimentary assessment of her coiffure. "And what's *that* supposed to mean?"

"What's...what...supposed to mean?" The facility with language that had served him so well in the legal profession seemed to have deserted him. So, too, had the ability to think quickly and clearly on his feet.

"Your claiming to have spent a lot of years 'visualizing' me."

"My *claiming?*" Chris stiffened with indignation. "I say you've been on my mind, and you accuse me of *making it up?*"

There was a fractious silence.

"No," Lucy finally said. There was an odd edge to her voice. She looked as though she'd flushed, but the lighting was too iffy to tell for sure. "That's *not* what you said."

"Excuse me?"

"You didn't say I'd been on your mind, Chris. You said you'd been visualizing me."

"It's the same thing."

"No, it's not." His ex-wife shook her head, her hair rippling about her face. The urge to touch the thick, dark tresses itched in the tips of Chris's fingers. He clenched his hands, willing the sensation to go away. "Visualizing someone is something you decide to do. It's intentional. But having someone on your mind...well, that's not necessarily a voluntary situation. You can't always help it."

Chris took a deep breath. Maybe Lucy had a point, he conceded. Maybe she didn't. Whatever the case, he didn't want to argue about it. Not here. Not now.

"Fine." He unclenched his fingers and made a conciliatory gesture. "Forget the visualizing. It was a bad choice of words. I've *thought* about you on and off during the last ten years. And when I've thought about you—sometimes intentionally, sometimes not—I've gotten an image inside my head. And until a minute ago, that image had long hair. The next time I think about you, the image will probably have—uh...uh...uh..."

"Not-so-long hair?"

Chris controlled a grimace at the undercurrent of quintessentially feminine sarcasm. All right. All right. So he wasn't fluent in fashionese. "I suppose," he said after a moment. "More or less."

There was a pause. A gust of wind sent a lock of Lucy's not-so-long hair fluttering across her cheek. She brushed it back. It pleased Chris to note that her manicured fingers did not appear to be entirely steady. Ignoble though it might be, he didn't like the sense of being the only one who was feeling off-balance in this situation.

And then, the inevitable question: "What are you doing here, Chris?"

He hesitated. He'd intended to be as up-front as possible with Lucy once he finally made contact with her. To tell her about his chance meeting with her former maid of honor and to explain the reasons behind his subsequent determination to seek her out after all these years. But considering how things had gone thus far...

Lord! She'd probably accuse him of stalking her. Or worse. And given the way he'd violated her trust more than a decade ago, he couldn't very well fault her for regarding his actions with suspicion.

"Here in Atlanta, you mean?" He didn't want to lie. Unfortunately, he couldn't quite see his way clear to telling the truth, the whole truth and nothing but the truth, either. Not under the circumstances.

Lucy nodded, thrusting her ungloved hands into the pockets of her coat.

"I came in on business yesterday. I was supposed to fly out late this afternoon, but there are weather problems on the other end."

"So you're . . . stranded?"

"Temporarily. I'll try to head home tomorrow."

"I see."

Chris cleared his throat. So much for the easy stuff, he thought. The stuff he could finesse without resorting to falsehood. But any second now, Lucy was going to hit him with the big one. Specifically, she was going to want to know how he'd just happened to turn up in front of the building in which she worked on what would have been their eleventh wedding anniversary.

Assuming that complete candor was not an option, what was he supposed to tell her? That fate must have conspired to bring them together again?

Oh, sure. Right.

Although . . .

There *was* something serendipitous about the way things had worked out, Chris reflected suddenly. Had he gone into Gulliver's Travels and found Lucy still on the job, that would have been one thing. But they'd *collided* with each other! What were the odds of that happening?

Had he arrived a minute or two later . . .

Had she departed a minute or two earlier . . .

They wouldn't have connected. At least not tonight.

Lucy started to open her mouth, clearly about to press her interrogation. Chris preempted her by asking, "What about you?"

She blinked. "What about me?"

"What are *you* doing here?"

He watched an unsettled combination of emotions streak across her expressive face. His breath snagged in his chest as a disturbing possibility occurred to him. *Damn!* What if Lucy had spoken with Tina Palucci? What if she knew that he knew what her current situation was?

No, he told himself a moment later. If Lucy had heard about his meeting with her one-time best friend, she would have countered the question he'd just asked with that fact. Because whatever her faults—and even in the first, deliri-

ously happy days of their marriage he hadn't deluded himself that his bride was free of human flaws and foibles—
Lucia Annette Falco wasn't into playing cat-and-mouse
games with the truth.

At least she hadn't been, he amended with a pang. Ten
years was a long time. Supposing—

"I live here." Lucy's crisp response disrupted his troubled line of conjecture. "In Atlanta, that is. But not in this
building. This is where I work." She lifted her chin. "I'm
office manager for an agency called Gulliver's Travels."

"Really?" Chris ventured a smile. She wasn't jerking him
around, he decided. The pride in her voice and expression
was too genuine. "Sounds challenging."

Lucy took a moment, seeming to weigh the sincerity of his
reaction. Then, slowly, her lips started to curve upward. Her
dimples indented for a heady half second. Chris's pulse
spurted at the sight. While he hadn't forgotten how very
lovely her smile was, memory was a pallid substitute for the
real thing.

"It is," she told him. "Very."

There was another pause. They just stood there on the
sidewalk. Still. Silent. Staring at each other. Then the wind
kicked up. Despite his earlier comment to the hotel concierge, Chris shivered. He saw the woman who had once
been his wife do the same.

"Are you in a hurry to get somewhere?" he asked
abruptly.

Lucy pulled a hand from her coat pocket and swatted at
her hair. Then she gave what apparently was meant to be a
casual little laugh. "It's New Year's Eve, Chris."

The implication of this statement was as obvious as the
laugh had been artificial. But just because it was obvious,
that didn't mean that Chris was going to accept it.

"Meaning what?" he pressed. "You have a date?"

Lucy's gaze held his for another moment, then skittered
away. He knew she was tempted to lie. He was also willing
to lay odds that she wouldn't.

"Lucy?"

"No," she said flatly, still not looking at him. "I don't have a date."

"How about a husband waiting at home?" He was ninety-nine and nine-tenths percent certain that there wasn't. Had his ex-wife made a second marriage—particularly a happy second marriage—the former Tina Roberts undoubtedly would have shoved the news down his throat and enjoyed watching him choke on it.

Her eyes slewed back to his. The flash of temper he saw in their depths told him he'd hit a nerve. But that was all it told him. *"No."*

"So?"

Lucy moistened her lips, plainly waging some kind of internal battle. Finally she countered, "What about you?"

"Me?"

"Did your getting stuck here in Atlanta put a crimp in your holiday plans?"

Chris felt his mouth twist. He wondered fleetingly how his ex-wife would react if he informed her that he'd spent what would have been their first two wedding anniversaries drinking himself into a stupor. He'd abandoned alcohol for work in subsequent years. Burying himself in legal files had proved almost as effective at holding memories at bay as guzzling booze. And when all was said and done, eyestrain and paper cuts were easier to cope with than a killer hangover.

"Not that you'd notice," he said flatly.

"No...date?"

"No. And no wife, waiting or otherwise." He let a few seconds tick by, then added, "I'm not really big on New Year's Eve celebrations anymore."

Lucy glanced down, her jaw working. After what seemed like a very long time, she quietly confessed, "Neither am I."

Chris released a breath he hadn't known he had been holding.

"What do you say we go someplace warm and get a drink?" he suggested, ruthlessly suppressing an urge to underscore the invitation with a touch. He told himself that he had to proceed very, very carefully. The territory he was in was strewn with psychological land mines. And while the brunette standing before him seemed breathtakingly familiar in some ways, she was very much a stranger in others. He couldn't make assumptions about anything where she was concerned, including her receptivity to physical contact.

"Now?"

He nodded.

"Why?"

Lord. How was he supposed to answer *that?*

"Auld lang syne?" he offered after a moment, sidestepping potentially explosive explanations.

"I don't know...."

"One drink, Lucy. No strings attached."

She nailed him with a formidable look. "With nearly ten years and a divorce decree between us? I should think not."

Chris swallowed hard, sensing that he was one—maybe two—wrong words from provoking his ex-wife into turning her back on him and walking away. The possibility shook him in ways he couldn't have begun to describe.

"Please?" he said in a low voice.

Lucy lowered her lashes, veiling her dark eyes. After a few seconds, she lifted them. "All right, Chris," she agreed, meeting his gaze once again. "There's a place just down the street we can go. One drink. No strings. And since this is my town, it's my treat."

They wound up on opposite sides of a small table tucked in a comparatively quiet corner of a hotel bar located a few blocks from Gulliver's Travels.

Although she'd picked the place and made it clear that she was going to pay for the drinks, Chris controlled the conversation from the moment they sat down. But he did it so subtly that Lucy didn't figure out what was going on until *after* she'd finished recounting how she'd come to be the office manager of Gulliver's Travels and launched into an enthusiastic description of the job she did and the unusual collection of people with whom she did it.

By then . . . well, it wasn't too late for her to stop talking. She could have shut up about herself and what she'd done since their divorce. She could have put her ex-husband on notice that she was wise to his manipulative behavior, as well. Only she didn't.

She didn't because she wanted Chris to understand what kind of woman she'd become since he'd last seen her. She wanted him to recognize that she'd changed a lot more than her hairstyle during the past decade.

That there was a nasty element of "Nyah-nyah-nyah, see how well I've done without you" fueling her protracted monologue, Lucy couldn't have denied. She was only human. It pleased her to have accomplishments to brag about, just as it pleased her to know that the wine-colored wool dress she was wearing just happened to be one of the most becoming garments in her wardrobe. Still, her mean-spirited desire to flaunt and taunt grew weaker and weaker the longer she spoke.

It did so because her ex-husband made it clear that he was impressed by what he was hearing. He nodded in all the right places, his eyes never wavering from hers. He leaned forward several times, as though wanting to make certain that he caught every nuance of what she was telling him. He also asked a lot of perceptive questions.

Questions about the business degree she'd finally earned a year after their split.

Questions about the entry-level job she'd landed with the office that oversaw Chicago's thriving tourist and convention trade and how she'd leveraged it into a position with a medium-size travel agency.

Questions about the way she'd climbed the ranks at the agency, mastering the ins and outs of organizing complicated trips, pleasing picky customers and keeping up with the massive amount of paperwork imposed by various and sundry local, state and federal bureaucracies.

Questions about how an impulsive response to an ad in the employment opportunities section of a leisure industry publication had led to her job with Gulliver's Travels.

No one in her family had ever asked her such questions. None of her friends, either. Oh, sure, her onetime maid of honor and postdivorce cheerleader inquired about her work whenever they spoke. But Lucy knew that Tina—now Mrs. Scott "Chachi" Palucci!—wasn't really that interested.

She didn't need Chris's approval, she assured herself as her ex-husband smiled his endorsement of the way she'd handled her initial employment interview with the formidable owner of Gulliver's Travels. Still, she had to admit that it was extraordinarily sweet to receive it.

Chris had paid attention to her in the past, of course. Indeed, she'd found the way he listened to her during their courtship to be remarkably erotic. She'd been accustomed to men who tended to discount the importance of women's conversations. To state her opinion on a subject and not have it brushed off with a patronizing "Yeah, yeah, I hear what you're tellin' me, babe" had had a startling effect on her libido.

But there was one big difference between then and now, Lucy reflected with a flash of painfully acquired self-knowledge. Back then, she'd harbored some serious doubts about the value of what she had to say.

She didn't harbor any such doubts now. While she was as prone to an occasional bout of insecurity as the next person, she was certain of her worth.

"I think we've gotten our roles reversed," she finally observed, fingering the stem of her almost emptied wineglass. She'd ordered her usual, the house white. She had no memory of having drunk any of it.

Chris cocked an eyebrow. He'd asked for Scotch on the rocks. The glass in front of him was almost untouched, the ice cubes it contained nearly melted. "What do you mean?"

"The girl's supposed to get the guy to talk about himself and his work, not vice versa." It was an oblique way of letting him know that she was aware of what he'd been up to. A sudden glint in his gray-green eyes told her that he'd gotten the message. It also sent a frisson of physical awareness prickling up her spine.

"When did you start subscribing to gender stereotypes?"

"Oh..." She gestured, trying to ignore the sexual energy that was coursing through her body like an electrical current. "...I've been known to make use of them every once in while."

"Ah, yes." Chris's gaze flicked from her face to her breasts and back again. Lucy shifted involuntarily and crossed her legs, acutely conscious of the sleek glide of her slip over her panty-hosed thighs. "I seem to recall you expounding about that on several occasions."

"A girl's gotta do what a girl's gotta do," she paraphrased, wary of starting a walk down memory lane. Although she knew that their shared past was ripe for review, it was better—*safer*—to stick with a discussion of the present.

"Mmm..." Her ex-husband took a sip of his drink. "Tell me more about this seldom-seen boss of yours, John Gulliver. He sounds a little like the mysterious employer in that old TV series, 'Charlie's Angels.'"

"Uh-uh." She shook her head decisively, determined to reverse the conversational flow and defuse the attraction she was feeling. "It's time to talk about you. What's the business that brought you to Atlanta?"

It seemed to her to be a very straightforward question. Hardly the kind of query that necessitated a lot of thought. But Chris lowered the glass slowly back to the table, appearing to weigh his answer very carefully. Finally he said, "I'm considering a job offer."

Lucy gasped as the implications of this quietly uttered statement sank in. *"H-here?"*

"I've been asked to become executive legal counsel to..." He named a well-known philanthropic organization.

"That's quite a departure from being a partner in a high-powered New York law firm!"

The blurted-out words seemed to hang in the air over the table. Lucy would have given just about anything to be able to pluck them down and jam them back into her mouth.

"And just what do you know about my being a partner in a high-powered New York law firm?" Chris queried after a few keenly uncomfortable seconds.

Lucy grimaced inwardly, cursing her wayward tongue. She'd always been prone to blabbing first and thinking through later. Her verbal impulsiveness had been a source of contention during her marriage. Although Chris had professed to admire her penchant for speaking her mind, she knew there'd been occasions when he felt she'd gone over the line.

"There was an article about you in the *New York Times* a few weeks back," she admitted stiffly. "Gulliver's Travels booked a couple on a cruise that turned out to be a front for a drug-smuggling ring. Everything worked out in the end, thank God. I mean, the couple came through the mess safely and the bad guys were busted. The *Times* has given the case a fair amount of coverage. Which, because of the agency's involvement, I've tried to follow. One of the stories jumped to a page in the business section that happened to have a photograph of you. There was a profile underneath. I...skimmed...it."

"I see." The response was mild to the point of seeming indifferent. It also sounded more than a little superior.

Damn him! Lucy thought, her anger at herself veering off toward her ex-husband. There had been a time when Chris's cool, self-contained style intrigued her. In the beginning, it had been the contrast with her own rather volatile temperament that compelled her interest. Later, it had been the erotic kick of knowing that as buttoned-down as Chris appeared in public, he was more than capable of letting it all hang out when the two of them were alone together behind closed doors.

She'd gone into her marriage confident that, despite his tendency to hold himself aloof from other people, Chris would open up to her without reservation. And for a while she'd believed that he was. But as the halcyon haze of honeymoon bliss gave way to everyday reality, she'd begun to suspect that she'd been deceived.

Even at their moments of greatest intimacy, when she felt her own identity and independence slipping away, she'd been plagued by the nagging fear that some part of Christopher Dodson Banks remained impervious to her. No matter how much she'd given. No matter how hard she'd tried to make herself into what she thought he wanted her to be. It had never seemed to be enough. Something about him seemed to stay just...out...of...reach.

"I haven't been keeping tabs on you!" she insisted. It was the truth. Unfortunately, the natural corollary—that she hadn't given a damn what had happened to him after their split—was rather less valid.

"With nearly ten years and a divorce decree between us?" her ex-husband shot back, without missing a beat. "I should think not."

Four

Lucy recognized the words as her own, of course. Her temper spiking into the red zone, she scooted back her chair and started to get up.

"This was a mistake," she announced, reaching for her purse. "I'm out of here. Happy New Year. Have a swell life."

"No!" Chris leaned across the table and snagged her wrist.

She tried to pull free. His grip tightened to the bruising point. His lean build and gentlemanly demeanor made it easy to underestimate his physical strength. Her mind flashed back to a night when her brothers had maneuvered him into helping them unload a truckful of supplies at the restaurant. Chris had matched her bulked-up siblings move for move and barely broken a sweat. Vinnie, Joey and Mikey had been openly impressed.

"Let go of me!" she demanded, shoving the memory away.

"I'm sorry."

Lucy froze, her breath backing up, at the tone of this apology. It was the same tone Chris had used when he uttered the word *please* in connection with his attempt to persuade her to have a drink with him. It was fierce with feeling, yet very, very vulnerable.

She'd never heard him speak in such a manner until this evening. Not even in the throes of sexual ecstasy, when he'd cried out his need for her in hoarse, barely understandable syllables. If truth be told, she'd come to believe that he couldn't. Or wouldn't. At least not within her hearing.

Maybe he'd spoken that way to the woman in whose arms she'd found him ten days before the first anniversary of their wedding. Lucy didn't know. She'd never asked. She'd told herself that there was no point in finding out. Betrayal was betrayal, no *if*s, *and*s, *but*s or mitigating explanations. Her father, brothers, uncles and cousins had backed her up, citing Falco family honor with a fervor that suggested they were immigrants just off the boat from vendetta-prone Sicily rather than second- and third-generation Americans with roots in the Lombardy region of northern Italy.

But now...

"Sorry for what?" she questioned, managing to keep her voice steady. She wished she could do the same with her heartbeat. She wondered whether Chris could feel the herk-jerk of her pulse.

"Would you like a list?"

"Do you have one?"

His mouth thinned. His gray-green eyes clouded with emotion. "Can you spare a day or two to listen?"

Lucy exhaled on a shaky breath. Her knees started to wobble. *"Chris—"*

"Something I can do for you folks?"

The query came from their server, a spiffily dressed young man with ponytailed hair and a gold ear stud. Although his manner was polite, something about his stance suggested that he'd hustled over to their table because he scented trouble.

Lucy felt Chris release her wrist. She sank back down into her seat, giving the waiter a quick smile. "No, thank you."

"A refill on your white wine, maybe?"

"I'm fine."

"Another Scotch, sir?"

"No, thanks."

"Would you bring the check, please?" Lucy requested after a moment.

The young man hesitated, his gaze flicking assessingly from one side of the table to the other. Finally he inclined his head and said, "Right away, ma'am."

"I guess the sparks were a little obvious," Chris observed with an edgy laugh after the waiter moved away.

Lucy felt a tinge of heat enter her cheeks. "Apparently so," she replied, flexing her wrist and glancing away.

A few seconds ticked by.

"About your asking for the check—"

She brought her gaze back to her ex-husband's face. She noted, not for the first time that evening, that the passage of time had barely touched him. A few new wrinkles at the outer corners of his eyes. A slight deepening of the lines that bracketed his mouth. Maybe a couple of silver strands at his temples. But aside from that, Chris looked much as he had the first time she caught sight of him.

"We agreed to have *one* drink," she pointed out.

Chris's well-shaped lips twisted. "That we did. And with no strings attached."

She lowered her gaze and began fiddling with the stem of her wineglass again. The hum of physical attraction was still there. It was a far cry from the incendiary desire that had once come close to consuming her, to be sure, but it was more seductive than anything she'd felt since her divorce.

Which was not to say that she'd had her libido on hold for the past decade. She was a normal, healthy woman with normal, healthy appetites, for heaven's sake. She'd dated.

She'd gone to bed with several attractive, eligible men. She'd even discussed the possibility of moving in with one of them. But when it came down to making a commitment, she'd pulled back. There had been something . . . missing.

There had been something missing from her marriage, as well, of course. Particularly at the end. And who knew? Maybe in the beginning, too. That was one of the thoughts that had been going around and around in her head as her certainties about what had happened between her and Chris slipped away.

"I *am* sorry," Chris asserted quietly, drawing her eyes once again.

"Oh?"

"For the crack about the nearly ten years and the divorce decree. It was totally uncalled-for."

She gave a ragged little laugh. "I said it first."

"True. But you're entitled."

"Entitled?"

"To take a shot at me. Or shots."

"You . . . think?" Lucy's heart performed a curious hop-skip-jump.

"Don't you?"

Of course she did! He'd broken the wedding vows he'd taken and shattered the happily-ever-after resolution they'd made. *And yet—*

"It was a long time ago, Chris."

"The past is over and done with, don't rake it up?"

Lucy licked her lips, buffeted by a series of contradictory emotions. Finally she sighed and said, "Not tonight."

Her ex-husband studied her silently for several moments, then nodded his head in apparent acquiescence to her wishes. "All right."

Their waiter returned with the bill. Lucy retrieved her purse, opened it, extracted her wallet and took out a credit card.

"Be back in a sec," the young man promised, bustling away.

"Were you serious before?" Lucy asked. "About the job offer from the foundation?"

"Very much so."

"What do your parents think?" It was a dicey question. To say that her wedding-night confidence about being able to come to terms with her blue-blooded in-laws had proved misplaced would be to understate the case. Still, she was curious.

Chris picked up the glass of watery Scotch, took a long drink, then set it down with a *clunk*. "I haven't the faintest idea."

"You haven't told them?"

"When did you tell your family you were contemplating going to work for Gulliver's Travels?"

Lucy flushed, remembering the scene. She also realized she'd been put on notice that, although her ex-husband might consider her "entitled" to take shots at him, he wasn't declaring open season on his mother and father. She could accept that. Respect it, even. The importance of family loyalty had been drummed into her from infancy. For all that her father, brothers, uncles and cousins might drive her stark raving crazy on occasion, she'd defend them to the death against outsiders.

"After the fact," she admitted, grimacing.

"*After* the fact?" Chris looked shocked. "What did you do, Lucy? Send them a change-of-address card?"

"Of course not!" Which wasn't to say that there hadn't been moments when she secretly wished that she could have found the nerve to opt for such a no-holds-barred assertion of her independence. "I told them after I'd agreed to take the job."

"But before you moved to Atlanta."

"Yes."

"How did they take the news?"

"Compared to what?" The way they'd taken the news that she was getting married, maybe? Or how about the way they'd taken the news that she was filing for divorce?

"Lucy—"

"You don't really want to know, Chris."

He tilted his head, a frown line appearing between his sandy-brown eyebrows. "I can understand them not wanting you to leave Chicago," he commented slowly. "But weren't they—aren't they—proud of your professional success?"

"Of course they're proud." What was she supposed to say? That he'd been more supportive of her ambitions in the space of one no-strings drink than her relatives had been during an entire decade? "They just have trouble expressing how—"

"Here we go," their waiter announced, swooping in with a credit-card slip and a pen.

"Thank you," Lucy said, grateful for the interruption. She checked the addition on the bill, tacked on a generous tip, then signed her name with a flourish. After separating off her receipt and the accompanying carbons, she handed the remaining portion of the credit slip and the pen back to the server.

"Thank *you*, ma'am!" the young man said with a broad grin. "And have a very happy New Year."

"Forty percent of the bill?" Chris asked in a teasing undertone as the waiter moved away. "That's a little over-the-top, even for you."

Lucy refused to rise to what was very familiar bait. "I appreciate good service."

"You mean you empathize with people who have to spend their holidays waiting tables."

"Having done it myself, yes." She smiled wryly, recalling the long days she'd spent schlepping food and beverages at her family's restaurant. She also recalled having seen Elizabeth Banks's impeccably lipsticked mouth compress into an unpleasant line when she talked about that experience. "But to tell the truth, it's more than that these days. The buzz in the travel biz is that women are lousy tippers."

"And you're bent on proving that's a vile canard."

"Well..."

Chris laughed. Not mockingly. Quite the contrary. The sound was warm. Almost...tender. It sent a quiver dancing through Lucy's nervous system. Her gaze met and mated with her ex-husband's. For a breathless moment, everything seemed to stand still.

"Lucy—" Chris began, the humor fading from his expression.

"It's time to go," she said quickly, looking away. She got to her feet and began collecting her things. Her hands were only marginally steadier than her pulse and breathing pattern.

She wondered later whether she'd wanted Chris to press her—perhaps even to plead with her—to stay. She could never say for sure. That she might have taken pleasure in making her ex-husband grovel for her company was not a particularly edifying thing to contemplate. Still...

There was no denying that she felt a pang of disappointment when Chris abandoned whatever he'd been about to say and stood up.

"So, tell me," he began in a casual tone, retrieving the classic tan trench coat he'd draped over the back of his chair before they sat down. His taste in clothes didn't seem to have altered much in ten years. She'd felt a definite rush of sartorial déjà vu when he unbuttoned the trench coat and revealed that he was wearing a midnight-blue suit, white shirt and burgundy silk tie. "What would you being doing right now if we hadn't run into each other?"

Lucy shrugged into her own coat, a black cashmere wrap she'd purchased on sale the previous winter. While she was happy to overtip, the thought of paying full retail price for clothing was anathema to her.

"Oh, I'd probably be curled up on my living room sofa with a bunch of—" She broke off, frowning.

"Lucy?"

She glanced around with a sense of dismay, then looked across the table and asked, "Did I have bunch of files with me when I came in here?"

Chris considered for a moment, then shook his head. "No. I don't think so. Why?"

"Damn." She expelled a frustrated breath. "I had a stack of work I was going to take home with me. I must've left it on my desk when I rushed out of the office."

"Rushed out?" The inflection of the question was odd.

Lucy made a face. "I was escaping from the telephone."

"Oh?"

"I thought it might be Joey or Mikey. Or one of my uncles."

"You weren't in the mood for New Year's greetings from your family?"

"Something like that." She clicked her tongue and took a quick look at her watch. After the shock of realizing that she'd been talking to her ex-husband for more than three hours faded, she came to a decision. "I'm going to go back."

"Now?"

"It's barely nine, Chris. If I don't go back tonight, I'll have to come in tomorrow morning."

"You're going to—what? Walk to the office?"

"It's not like it's a ten-mile trek across freezing tundra."

"And then what? Do you have a car?"

"Yes, but I took MARTA in today."

"The subway?"

She nodded, wondering why Chris was asking so many questions. Surely he didn't doubt that she was capable of getting herself from here to there and home in one piece. Travel was her profession, for heaven's sake!

She suddenly recalled the yellow cab she'd glimpsed earlier. "Maybe I'll call a taxi from the office. The agency has an account with one of the local services."

"No," her ex-husband said.

"Excuse me?"

"I have a better—*another*—idea."

Lucy gave him points for the amendment. Few things got her back up more quickly than a man assuming that any scheme that came out of his head was ipso facto superior to any notion of hers.

"Yes?" she prompted after a moment or two.

"We can get a cab here at the hotel. The driver can take us to your office so you can pick up your files. Then he can take you home and me to my hotel."

Lucy felt a sudden fluttering deep in her stomach. Was this some kind of ploy? she wondered uneasily. Had Chris picked up on the response his unexpected reappearance had evoked in her? Was he figuring that she'd feel... compelled... to ask him in once they arrived at her town house?

"Why don't we get two cabs and go our separate ways?" she countered, cocking her chin. The possibility that her ex-husband might perceive her as some sort of sexual push-over rankled at a very visceral level.

"Because I'd like to make certain you get safely inside your door."

He sounded sincere, she thought. And the expression in his eyes seemed very straightforward. But how could she—

"Lucy." Chris had moved from his side of the table. Although he wasn't crowding her, he was close enough so she could catch a whiff of his cologne. Her instinct was to step back. But this instinct was overridden when he lifted his hand and brushed his fingertips very gently against her hair. His touch was feather-light, barely stirring the dark strands. "Please. I'm not envisioning pushing my way into your home. I'll stay in the taxi while you go into your office. I'll stay in the taxi while you go into your house. I'll sit in front with the damned driver, if that's what you want. I'd just like to start this particular New Year knowing that you're all right."

No, he wasn't crazy, Lucy reflected, her toes curling in-side her black calfskin pumps. But there was a fair-tomiddling possibility that she was on the verge of losing her own grip on reality.

"Okay, " she agreed throatily. "You don't have to sit in the front seat. But you do have to promise to stay in the taxi."

"I know what I promised," Chris said to Lucy as their cab came to a halt in front of the Gulliver's Travels office building a short time later. "But would it be okay if I came in with you?"

His ex-wife cocked an eyebrow, her expression wary. He clamped down on a spurt of anger at her continued suspiciousness. She had cause to doubt him, he reminded himself grimly.

"Why?" she asked after a moment.

"Nature calls. I need to use a rest room." It was the truth.

"Oh." An expression he couldn't read flickered across her face.

"And I wouldn't mind a quick tour of where you work." This was the truth, too.

Lucy studied him silently for a moment or two, then nodded. "Okay."

"Good."

"Whoa, man, whoa!" their driver cried as she started to open the door. He turned around, his gaze bouncing back and forth between them. "You *both* goin' inside?"

"We won't be long," Lucy said quickly. "Five minutes at the most."

The cabbie was not soothed by this. Fixing his eyes on Chris, he demanded, "What 'bout my money, then?"

"What about it?"

"How do I know this ain't some scam? How do I know you two ain't plannin' to sneak out of that buildin' some back way I can't see and leave me whistlin' for my fare? Huh? Tell me that, man. How do I know?"

The driver had a point, Chris conceded to himself. A point that impugned his and Lucy's integrity, to be sure, but a point nonetheless. He glanced at his former wife. She'd let go of the door handle and was reaching for her purse.

"No," he said impulsively, placing a restraining hand on her arm. He felt a faint tremor of response. His own pulse accelerated in answer. Ten years, he thought, with the same combination of wonder and dismay that had engulfed him more than a couple of times in the hotel bar. Ten years, and their sexual chemistry was still very, very volatile.

"No?" she echoed, lifting her gaze to his.

He cleared his throat, removing his hand. "You bought the drinks. Let me pick up the cab fare."

"I can expense it, Chris."

"So can I."

"The meter's runnin'," the driver pointed out.

Lucy expelled a breath in a huffy little sigh and gave in. "Oh, all right."

Unbuttoning his trench coat, Chris reached inside his suit jacket and extracted his wallet. He flipped it open and removed several bills. He'd made a withdrawal from an ATM at Hartsfield Airport, and he was carrying more cash than he normally did.

"This is for the fare so far," he said, placing the money in the driver's upturned palm. "Plus another five to cover the time we're inside."

"If it runs out and you're not back, I'm gone," the cabbie warned, folding the cash and tucking it away. "This is a holiday night, man. Guys like me make big bucks *drivin'*, not hangin' around."

"Understood."

"We won't be long," Lucy stressed.

The driver cocked his head. "No tip?"

Chris bit back a suggestion that the guy not press his luck and plucked another five-dollar bill from his wallet. He forked it over.

The driver grinned avariciously, flashing a gold-sheathed front tooth. "Happy New Year, man."

Lucy opened the taxi door and got out. Chris slid across the seat and exited the cab, as well. He shivered. The temperature had dropped a good ten degrees in the past few hours. A light snow had begun to fall, dusting the sidewalk like a fine sprinkling of confectioners' sugar.

"I suppose you would've tipped the guy ten," Chris groused as he slammed the cab door.

"Nope." Lucy gave him a sassy smile. "I don't pay blackmail."

They crossed from the curb to the entrance of the building.

"The building locks up at six," Lucy reported as they came to a halt. Her breath condensed in the frigid air, issuing from her lips in a silvery mist. "The security guard will have to buzz us in."

Chris peered through one of the glass doors, surveying the lobby. "I see a security *desk*," he observed, aware that his need for a rest stop was growing more acute. "But no sign of a guard."

"Darn." Lucy tucked her hands up under her arms. "He must be making his rounds."

Figuring that there was no harm in trying, Chris grasped the metal handle of the door through which he'd been looking and pulled. The door yielded to his touch. He heard Lucy make a small, surprised sound.

"The plot thickens," he joked, gesturing her ahead of him.

"This isn't good," she commented with a frown as they stepped inside. "Tom could get in big trouble for not locking that door."

"Tom's the missing guard, I take it?" It didn't surprise him that she knew the man's name. Lucy had always made a point of personally connecting with easy-to-overlook people like night watchmen, waiters and hotel chambermaids.

"Uh-huh." She undid the tie belt of her coat. "He's new to the job, and kind of nervous about how he'll handle it."

"Well, if the unlocked door and unmanned desk are any indication, he's got a few things to learn."

They walked forward, their footsteps echoing in the empty lobby. Lucy suddenly checked herself in midstride, holding up her hand and tilting her head to one side.

"What?" Chris asked sharply, halting as well.

"Did you hear that? It sounded like—" she frowned "—*drilling*."

He cocked an ear and listened for a few seconds, but heard nothing that struck him as unusual. "No. Sorry."

Lucy glanced around then called out, "Tom? Can you hear me? It's Lucy Falco from Gulliver's Travels!"

No response.

"Do you want to forget this?" Chris asked after a moment or two. Although he did not consider himself a particularly intuitive person, he had an uneasy feeling about this foray.

"No." Lucy's refusal was quick, unequivocal, and accompanied by a decisive shake of her head. "I really need to pick up those files. Besides, I thought you wanted to use the—" She broke off, smacking her brow in a "Stupid me" gesture. "*I* know why Tom isn't at his desk. He must be upstairs with the repairmen!"

"The . . . repairmen?" The hit-to-the-forehead move was poignantly familiar. The sight of it made him remember the way he'd used to tease Lucy that if he ever genuinely wanted to deprive her of speech, he wouldn't gag her. He'd tie her hands.

"They arrived as I was on my way out. Just a few minutes before I bumped into you, as a matter of fact. There's some problem with the toilets on the third floor."

Chris allowed himself a fleeting moment to contemplate the concept of repairmen who were willing to work after hours on a holiday. After nearly eight years in New York, the idea was almost incomprehensible to him. Then he said slowly, "That could have been the noise you thought you heard."

Lucy endorsed this suggestion with a quick smile.

"I'm sure it was," she said. "In the meantime, we'd better get a move on, before our taxi driver decides to take off. The men's room is that way." She pointed. "And Gulliver's Travels is this way. Last door on the left."

Chris emerged from the john about two minutes later, his trench coat slung over his arm. He retraced his steps to the point where he and Lucy had separated, then headed down the corridor she'd taken. He noted that the last door on the left was slightly ajar.

He opened his mouth to call out Lucy's name.

And then he heard it. Not drilling. No, indeed not. What he heard was a muffled thud, followed by what sounded like a very human yelp of distress.

Chris had been a champion sprinter in high school. Fast-off-the-mark instincts kicked in, fueled by a rush of adrenaline. He cast his coat aside and started running.

Lucy, he thought. *If something's happened to Lucy—*

He skidded to a halt in front of the last door on the left and flung it open. Then he charged inside.

He saw two thugs. One mustachioed and wearing mud brown. The other burly, bearded, and clad in dark blue.

They were attacking Lucy!

"You bastards!" he roared, ready to kill.

"Chris!" his ex-wife cried, kicking at her assailants. "Look out!"

Look out? Look out for what?

A split second later, something wielded by someone clouted the back of his skull.

Christopher Dodson Banks saw stars.

Then he saw nothing at all.

Five

Lucia Annette Falco's life had prepared her to cope with a lot of different situations. Unfortunately, being stashed in a storage room after having been bound around the wrists and ankles with duct tape and tied back-to-back with her temporarily insensible former spouse was not one of them.

To put it bluntly, she didn't know whether to laugh, cry or scream her head off. Alternating between the three had a certain appeal. So, too, did trying to do all three simultaneously.

She'd worked herself into quite a state by the time Chris regained consciousness. While anxiety about his condition was the primary reason for her upset, guilt was a close second.

This is my fault, she thought, staring miserably at the stuff-crammed shelves that lined the small storage room. She was sitting with her back to the door. Her companion in captivity was facing it. *If only I hadn't been so insistent on coming back to get my files . . .*

There was nothing in those files that required her immediate attention, and she knew it. She could have left them sitting on her desk until after the start of the New Year with a clear conscience. But, *noooo*... She'd wanted to impress Chris with the heaviness of her work load and the dedicated professionalism with which she bore it.

See how indispensable I am! she'd been trying to communicate. *I may have been a pizza parlor cashier without a college degree the first time you laid eyes on me, but I've made myself into the linchpin employee of a very successful business with a worldwide reach!*

Gritting her teeth, Lucy strained against the bindings on her wrists and ankles. They didn't give. She then tried struggling against the ties that had her rubbing spines with her unconscious ex-husband. They didn't give, either.

Damn!

She returned to her exercise in self-flagellation.

While her ploy with the files had been bad enough, her surrender to Chris's let's-share-a-cab proposal had been even worse, she reflected. If only she'd stuck by her guns and gone her separate way!

She understood what had prompted her acquiescence, of course. She'd wanted to prolong their time together. Never mind her misgivings about Chris's reasons for desiring to see her to her door for the first time in more than a decade. Deep down, she hadn't been ready to say goodbye to him again. Deep down inside, she'd felt a need to—

The man she was tethered to stirred, gave a guttural groan, then stirred again.

"Chris?" She invoked the name as if it were a prayer.

There was more stirring, followed by yet another groan. Then, uncertainly: "L-Lucy?"

Tears threatened. She blinked them back. Relief sluiced through her, sweeping away a lot of emotional debris.

"Uh-huh," she managed to affirm. Then, instinctively trying to lighten the moment, she asked, "Do you wish you'd stayed in the taxi?"

Chris made a sound that was midway between a chuckle and a gasp. "Oh...God," he said, shifting his position. The movement felt awkward to Lucy, as though he were having trouble getting his brain and body in sync. "Please. Don't make me laugh."

"Are you okay?" she questioned, desperately wishing she could get a look at his face. She'd pleaded with their captors not to tie them back-to-back, but they'd insisted that that was how it had to be done.

"*Okay* is a relative term."

"Chris—"

"I'm conscious. I don't seem to be bleeding. I can wiggle my fingers and toes."

"Do you think you might have a concussion?" She'd tormented herself with this possibility all the time he'd been out. Phrases she'd picked up from TV medical shows—like *subdural hematoma*—had echoed ominously through her brain.

"I doubt it. I have a very thick skull."

The self-deprecating comment struck a responsive chord, but Lucy ignored it. "Are you seeing double? Feeling dizzy or drowsy?"

"No."

"Well, if you start experiencing any weird symptoms—" She stopped, not wanting to finish the sentence.

"You'll be the second one to know. All I've got right now is a headache."

"Bad?"

Her ex-husband gave an odd, edgy laugh, as though remembering something he'd just as soon not. "I've had worse."

"Oh," she replied, feeling compelled to say something. She wished she could move her hands. She flashed briefly on a memory of Chris teasing her about how much she gestured when she spoke. She pushed the recollection away as quickly as she could. "I . . . I'm sorry."

There was a pause. Lucy felt Chris shift position again. Then he quietly asked, "Are *you* all right?"

The question surprised her. "Aside from being tied up and really, *really* ticked off, you mean?"

Another laugh from Chris. This one, unlike the one that preceded it, held a hint of genuine humor. "Yes."

"I'm fine."

"Those two thugs. They didn't try to...hurt...you?"

It took a moment for the implications of this carefully phrased query to sink in. Once it did, Lucy flushed. Was *that* why Chris had looked so murderous in the few moments before he was knocked senseless? she wondered with an involuntary shiver. Had he come charging to her rescue like the Seventh Cavalry because he thought that she was on the verge of being—

"No, Chris," she said hastily, feeling the heat in her face intensify. "They didn't hurt me. They roughed me up a little, but they weren't trying to...you know."

"Would you tell me if they had been?"

Lucy closed her eyes, hearing echoes of old arguments lurking beneath this query. She clenched her fingers, pushing the past away once again. She had to concentrate on the here and now.

"Yes," she said after a moment, reopening her eyes and staring straight ahead. "I would."

She heard what sounded like a sigh. "I hope so."

There was another pause. Lucy suddenly felt Chris's spine arch and the muscles of his upper back ripple and tense. She deduced that he was testing the strength of his bonds, much as she'd done a short time earlier. After a few seconds, she heard him exhale on a curse and knew he'd been frustrated in his bid to break free.

"Chris—"

"Do you have any idea what we stumbled into?"

"No," she frankly admitted. She'd been grabbed from behind a few moments after she stepped inside Gulliver's Travels and flicked on a light. She hadn't had a chance to register much. "Not really." Then she grimaced. "But I do know why the guard wasn't at the security desk."

"They've got him, too?"

"Uh...no." She grimaced a second time, guilt roiling up within her. She'd *known* that there was something off about Tom! She should have acted on that knowledge. She should have called the police. Or the security company. *Something*. "Not the way you mean."

"Are you saying—?"

"Yes. Unfortunately."

"The security guard is in on this?"

"Whatever 'this' is." The one thing she *had* noticed during the seconds before she was seized was that one of the office's walls had been stripped of its usual display of travel posters and defaced with spray paint. She'd seen a series of intersecting lines, a bunch of lopsided circles and several arrows. Also, an X. A large black X. What the significance of the spot it marked was, she had no idea.

"Was Tom the guy who tried to crack my skull open?"

"Actually...that was one of the repairmen."

"The alleged toilet-fixers?"

"Uh-huh. Tom's the one in brown. The repairmen have on the dark blue jumpsuits."

Chris expelled a breath. "I should have known," he muttered. "Repairmen who work after hours on a holiday? It had to be a scam."

"*You* should have known?" Lucy stiffened indignantly, jerking against the fetters on her wrists. She was not about to let him annex any responsibility for this debacle. "*I'm* the one who—"

She broke off when she heard the storage room door open.

"Ohmygod," Chris breathed.

Lucy's heart cartwheeled.

"What is it?" she demanded, frantically trying to shift her position. Her uncoordinated movements would have sent them both toppling over, if Chris hadn't counterbalanced by leaning in the opposite direction. By the time they were stabilized, Lucy no longer had her back to the door. But she still had to turn her head to find out what had prompted her ex-husband's reaction.

Ohmygod, indeed.

Their captors were lined up just inside the door. They were clad in the same clothing they'd had on earlier. They were also wearing masks.

And not just any masks, either. No, these were the Mardi Gras masks that Tiffany Tarrington Toulouse had purchased for the agency's promotional salute to New Orleans.

"Don't be s-scared," Tom the guard said from behind an elaborately spangled concoction of plume-bedecked plastic. He could hide his mustachioed face, but he couldn't hide his scrawny build or his baby-poop-brown uniform. "These masks are for your protection."

The utter absurdity of this assertion prompted Lucy to engage her mouth without consulting her brain. "Those masks are the property of Gulliver's Travels, Tom!"

"Lucy—" Chris warned in an undertone.

"Hey, why did you call him Tom?" This query came from the bearded repairman. He was sporting the alligator headpiece that Jimmy Burns had spoken about coveting.

"Because that's what he told me his name was."

Gator Head turned toward Glitter Mask. "You *told* her your name was Tom?"

"I needed an alias!"

"Oh, great! Just great! And who gave you permission to pick *my* name to be *your* alias? Huh? Huh? Huh?"

"I didn't p-pick it! It kind of... of... came out of my mouth before I knew it. She asked me what my name was, and I had to say *something*."

"That something didn't have to be *my* name! Jeez Louise, Dick—"

"His name is Dick?" Lucy interrupted, experiencing a peculiar feeling of déjà vu. This squabble reminded her of arguments she'd heard involving Vinnie, Joey, Mikey and the various Falco cousins. While she liked to think that her kinsmen's level of, er, *discussion* was a few IQ points above that of these two bozos, she couldn't deny that the juvenile sniping sounded very familiar.

The gator head swung in her direction, bobbing an emphatic affirmative. "That's right. *I'm* Tom. *He's* Dick. Tom and Dick Spivey."

Brothers. It figured.

"Oh, man!" This disgusted-sounding exclamation came from the third member of the trio, the balding repairman who'd knocked Chris out. He was sporting a smiley-face mask. "Why don't you go ahead and tell 'em who I am, too?"

In an act that surprised Lucy not a bit, Tom—the real one, not the plume-wearing usurper—accepted this obviously sarcastic suggestion at face value.

"His name's Percival Johnson," he announced.

Chris snorted, obviously trying to suppress a laugh. Lucy sympathized. There was a semihysterical giggle tickling at the back of her throat, too.

"Tom…Dick…and *P-Percival?*" her ex-husband asked.

Mr. Smiley-Face—a.k.a. Percival Johnson—took a step forward. Lucy's impulse toward merriment died as she remembered that this was the fellow who'd coshed Chris across the back of the skull.

She murmured her ex's name in an undertone, trying to nudge him with her elbow.

"You got a problem with Percival?"

Lucy felt Chris tense. He'd apparently realized that he'd crossed over some kind of line.

"Not at all," he responded politely. "It's a very… classic…name."

"That's because his mom was an English teacher," Tom put in helpfully.

Percival whirled on him. "You shut up about my mama!"

"Yeah, T-Tom," Dick seconded snidely. "Shut up. You know Butch don't like people talking about his mother!"

"Butch?"

Lucy and Chris blurted this out simultaneously. Then, in one of those weirdly spontaneous moments of absolute synchronicity, he twisted his head left and looked over his shoulder at her while she twisted her head right and looked over her shoulder at him. For a few neck-straining seconds, they literally saw eye-to-eye.

Lucy's heart was thudding like a tom-tom by the time those seconds ended. She was tingling clear down to her neatly pedicured toes.

"That's right," the maternally protective Percival growled. "I got nicknamed Butch in the slammer."

The tingling gave way to a sudden frisson of fear.

"You were in . . . prison?" Lucy tried not to think about the behavior patterns that might earn a convict the sobriquet *Butch*.

"That's where him and me met," Tom volunteered.

Oh, wonderful! *Two* of their captors had done time behind bars!

"I've never been in prison," Dick remarked, sounding a little sad.

"Yeah, well, that's because you're a wuss," Percival "Butch" Johnson snapped.

"I am not!"

"You are so!" This was from Tom.

"I am *not!*"

"Whaddya call not lockin' the front door to the building?" Butch demanded.

"That wasn't *wussy!* That was *forgetful!*"

"No, that was goddamned stupid! If you'd locked that front door, we wouldn't be stuck baby-sitting these two—"

"Hey, guys!" Chris's well-modulated voice cracked like a whip. The masked trio jumped. Even Lucy started. She'd never heard her ex-husband sound so aggressively commanding. "Can we cut the bickering and jump to the bottom line? *What are you doing here?*"

There was a long silence.

"I . . . I d-don't think we should tell you that," Dick finally said.

"Yeah," Tom concurred, his alligator headpiece bobbing. "It's none of your business."

"Excuse me?" Lucy said, her temper flaring. "I think people invading my travel agency is very much my business!"

"This place is yours?" Tom asked. "Wow!"

"Well—"

"No, it's not *hers,*" Dick put in crankily. "I told you before. Don't you ever pay attention? It belongs to some guy named Gulliver who never comes around. She works here. Her name's Lucy Something."

"Lucy?" Butch repeated. "Is that short for Lucille? I had a hound named Lucille once. God, I loved that dawg."

"Uh . . . no." Her brief flash of anger had subsided. "It's short for Lucia."

"Lucia?" It was Tom again. "You Eye-talian or something?"

"Or something," Chris replied flatly. "Lucy's family's been in America for several generations."

"Who the hell are you?" The question came from Butch.

"Yeah," Tom echoed. "Who the hell are you?"

"Yeah," Dick agreed. "We've all introduced ourselves. It's no fair if you don't, too."

For a moment, Lucy thought her ex-husband might balk. Then he said, "I'm Chris Banks."

Tom snickered. "Banks, like in money?"

"Not exactly."

A few seconds ticked by. Eventually Lucy said, "If you won't tell us what you're doing here, will you at least give us a hint about how long we're going to be stuck in this storage room?"

A few more seconds ticked by. The masked trio exchanged looks, plainly reluctant to respond.

"Tom? Dick? Uh . . . Butch?"

The first two dipped their heads. The third rose to the challenge. "Till sometime Thursday."

"Thursday?" Lucy assured herself that Butch must have misspoken. While he seemed to be the closest to a criminal mastermind this crew had, he also appeared to have more than a few fried brain circuits. "Are you talking the day after *tomorrow?"*

"It's not that long," Tom argued. "It's gettin' pretty close to midnight. Thursday'll be the day after today when it's Wednesday."

For an unnerving moment, Lucy thought this last statement sounded almost . . . lucid.

"What kind of heist takes nearly forty-eight hours?" Chris asked quietly.

"The kind where you have to drill through a concrete wall to get to a—" Dick broke off with an inarticulate cry of dismay, then lifted his right arm and pointed a shaking finger at Chris. "You *tricked* m-me!" He glanced at his criminal colleagues. "He *tricked* me into telling him that!"

"He sure as hell did," Butch said with a gravelly laugh, then flashed a thumbs-up signal. "Pretty slick move, Chris."

"Thanks, Butch."

Lucy couldn't believe her ears. What was this? she asked herself with a flash of very feminine irritation. A moment of buddy-buddy bonding, with Chris amiably accepting a compliment from the ex-convict who'd tried to crack his skull open?

Men!

Which wasn't to say that she disagreed with Butch's assessment of what Chris had done. Her ex-husband *had* pulled a shrewd one. Thanks to him, they now knew their captors were intent on drilling through a wall to—

Comprehension dawned. A fragment of her conversation with Wayne Dweck clicked with something Tom—uh, no, *Dick*—had let drop when they chatted at the security desk.

"The vault!" Lucy exclaimed. "You're breaking into that vault next door! The one that's full of...of...of..."

"The Red Treasure," Dick finished reverently.

"Yeah." Tom sighed. "The Red Treasure."

The Red Treasure? What the heck was the Red Treasure?

"Okay," Chris said after several suspenseful seconds. "I'll bite. What's the Red Treasure?"

"Cash money. Lots of it."

"Gold and jewels."

"A fortune in untraceable bearer bonds."

"Uh-huh." Lucy heard her ex-husband take a deep breath and release it in a long, slow God-give-me-patience sigh. "In other words, you're not sure."

"Well...no," Butch conceded, looking down at his feet. "Not exactly. But we've been hearing rumors about it. Whatever it is, it's priceless."

There was an awkward silence. During the course of it, Lucy actually found herself starting to feel a little sorry for Tom, Dick and Butch.

Yes, she realized that they were criminals. Yes, she was acutely aware that one of them had hit Chris over the head. She was likewise cognizant of the fact that that same individual had informed her she was going to be spending the rest of New Year's Eve and all of New Year's Day tied up in a storage room with her ex-husband.

Hmm... Maybe "feeling sorry" was a bit of an overstatement.

"What was that 'for our protection' thing you mentioned when you came in—" she took a beat to make certain she had the name straight "—Dick?"

"What?"

"When you and Tom and Butch first walked into the storage room, you said something about wearing masks for Chris's and my protection."

"Oh, yeah," Tom jumped in eagerly. "It's so's you can't see our faces and identify us later."

Lucy mulled this statement for several moments. No, she thought. No. There is no way these three could be *that* stupid.

Well . . .

Okay. Okay. Maybe Tom and Dick Spivey could be. But not Percival "Butch" Johnson.

"Guys," she said slowly. "I don't want to sound— I mean, I realize two of you have been to prison and are probably a lot more clued in on this kind of thing than me— but, uh, well . . . *we've already seen your faces.*"

Although this statement provoked no immediate response from the three men to whom it was addressed, it did earn her a sharp jab from Chris's left elbow.

"I mean, *I've* seen your faces," she quickly corrected, realizing that she'd done her ex-husband a potentially dangerous disservice by speaking in the plural. "Before. When I was leaving. Remember? You saw me. I saw you. In the lobby. But Chris couldn't have caught more than a glimpse of any of you before Butch knocked him out. And everyone knows a blow to the head can cause short-term memory—"

"Everyone *also* knows that eyewitnesses are notoriously unreliable when it comes to describing or identifying people," Chris cut in with ruthless precision. "And empirical studies have shown that being subjected to extreme stress— *like being manhandled and tied up in a storage room*—can have a deleterious impact on an individual's short-term memory, too."

"*Huh?*" Tom and Dick said simultaneously.

Butch gave another deep-in-the-chest chuckle. "Tell me, Chris," he drawled, "you wouldn't happen to be a lawyer, would you?"

"Harvard Law. Class of—"

"I knew it! The way you slipped that question in on Dick, I was ninety percent sure you were a mouthpiece. But hearin' you spout off just now—" Butch chuckled again. "You do any criminal stuff?"

"Corporate, mostly. And some *pro bono* work."

"Who's Pro Bono?" Tom asked, sotto voce.

"Some Eye-talian, I think," Dick replied with a shrug.

What does Chris think he's doing? Lucy wondered a bit wildly.

"But even with only minimal experience on the criminal side," her ex-husband went on without missing a beat, "I can tell you that whatever other laws you gentlemen may have broken this evening, those infractions are minor compared with taking Lucy and me hostage."

"Hostage?" Tom yelped.

"Oh, no, no," Dick rushed in. "You're not *hostages!* We don't want to trade you for anything! And we're not going to hurt you, either. Even if you *have* seen our faces. Because by the time you have the chance to tell *anyone* what we look like, we'll be long gone with the Red Treasure."

"He's right. You're not hostages. You're like our... guests!"

Lucy choked. *"Guests?"*

"Yeah, sure," Dick said, picking up Tom's assertion. "Maybe not totally, uh, willing ones—"

"And damned sure not expected ones, either, since you forgot to lock the door."

"I *said* I was sorry! Why do you keep picking on me about that, Butch?"

"Because you were stupid, stupid," Tom said cheerfully.

Dick whirled on him, quivering with indignation. "*I* was stupid? You want to talk stupid? Let's talk about who forgot to bring the groceries I went out and bought so we could have something to eat tonight and all day tomorrow. I spent nearly *sixty bucks,* Tom. All you had to do was remember to put the stuff in the car—"

"Shut *up!*" Butch yelled.

Dick did. Tom stayed quiet, too.

Lucy closed her eyes. She contemplated the possibility that none of this was real. Maybe she was dreaming. She'd had New Year's Eve dreams involving Chris before. Maybe this was just another one.

"You don't have any food?" she heard her ex-husband ask.

"We'll manage," Butch responded.

"Whatever you 'manage' might be easier with one less mouth to feed. Let me offer a suggestion. Let Lucy go."

It took the former Mrs. Christopher Dodson Banks a moment or two to process the last three words.

Let Lucy go.

Let Lucy—

Her eyelids flew open. She sat as bolt upright as her bonds would allow her. *"Let Lucy go?"* she repeated incredulously.

"No way!"

"She'd run to the police!"

"Not if you still had me."

There was a stark, stunned silence. Lucy jabbed her elbow into Chris, much as he'd jabbed his into her. He didn't seem to feel it.

"You two got somethin' goin', huh?" Butch finally asked.

"No!" Lucy denied.

"Yes," Chris confirmed.

Tom snickered through his alligator mask. "Sounds like true love to me."

"Is it yes or no?" Butch pressed. "I don't see any wedding rings."

"We used to be . . . married." Lucy forced the admission out through clenched teeth. She had no idea what her ex-husband thought he was playing at, but she had no intention of participating. When all was said and done, this was her mess, not his. "And as for his idea of your letting me go—forget about it. I won't leave."

"Lucy—" Chris began.

She twisted around as far as she could. "I *won't*, Chris!"

"Wait a minute," Dick said, sounding puzzled. "Lucy, you said 'used to' be married. Does that mean . . . not anymore?"

"We're divorced," Chris said without inflection.

"She's your *ex-wife?*" Butch's voice rose sharply. "You'd trust your *ex-wife* not to go running to the police so they'd move in with SWAT teams and blow all of us away, including you?"

"Jeez." Tom snorted. "If it was *my* ex-wife—"

Dick cut in. "Don't start bad-mouthing Dora-Jean."

"Why not? You divorced her, too. Twice."

"So? It doesn't mean I want to hear people sayin' nasty things about her."

"You were both married to the same woman?" Lucy's head was whirling. Somewhere in the back of her mind, she realized that Chris hadn't answered the question Butch had put to him. *Did* he trust her to such a degree? After everything that had happened between them? After ten years of going their separate ways?

"Not at the same time," Dick assured her.

"We went back and forth," Tom elaborated. "Him. Me. Him again. And he calls *me* stupid!"

"Damn you—"

"Shut up!" Butch bellowed, ripping off his smiley-face mask and throwing it on the floor. "We've wasted enough time in here. We've got a wall to get through and a vault to crack, and we don't have until next year to do it!"

Tom peeled up the alligator headpiece and started scratching his bearded chin. "You know, Butch," he said slowly. "We sorta do. Have till next year, I mean."

The balding man glared at him. "Which part didn't you understand, Tom? The *shut* or the *up?*"

"I understood both of 'em just fine. But you said it to Dick."

"He meant *both* of us, you idiot."

"Oh..."

Lucy felt Chris shift. She squirmed a little, too. Her bottom was beginning to get numb.

"Butch?" her ex-husband finally asked. "What do you say to letting Lucy go?"

"Absolutely not!" They'd have a fight on their hands if they tried to turn her loose, Lucy vowed furiously. They'd have to drag her out of the building, kicking and screaming. The struggle she'd put up earlier would look like a game of pattycake by comparison. *"I'm staying here with you, Chris!"*

"Well, Mr. Harvard Lawyer Banks," replied Percival Johnson. "I say my mama raised me to believe that when a lady says no, a gentleman has to respect it. Looks like you and your ex-missus are gonna see in the New Year together."

Six

Chris drew a long, slow breath as the storage room door clicked shut, leaving him and Lucy alone once again. He emptied his lungs in a carefully calibrated exhalation. *Stay calm,* he told himself, flexing and unflexing his fingers. *Stay cool.*

He didn't usually need to coach himself along these lines. Staying calm and cool—more or less detached from life—was pretty much second nature to him. Self-control had been bred into him from the cradle. It came easy.

Except with Lucy.

Lucia Annette Falco was like a force of nature. His life had unexpectedly intersected with hers eleven and a half years ago and...*kablooey.* Goodbye calm, cool Christopher Dodson Banks. Hello to a guy with raging hormones and a heart overflowing with emotions he could barely handle.

It had scared him. Oh, not at first. After he resolved his concerns that he might be using his involvement with Lucy to make some psychologically screwed-up point about who he was or wasn't, he'd pretty much given himself over to the roller-coaster ride. At least temporarily.

He'd been crazy in love, and he'd gloried in it. But once sanity began to reassert itself, he'd begun to get the jitters. He'd never wanted anyone the way he wanted Lucy. Never...*needed*...anyone with such intensity. Whether she'd asked for it or not, he'd ceded her enormous power over his life. The implications of his doing so had shaken him to the center of his soul.

He'd pulled back. He admitted that. Or maybe he should say he'd *tried* to pull back. Although Lucy had accused him of holding himself aloof from her during the last few months of their marriage, he'd always felt intensely engaged and dangerously vulnerable.

Chris closed his eyes, flashing back to the private words he and Lucy had exchanged just a few scant hours after they traded very public vows.

Eleven years ago, that had been. Eleven years, to this very night. Possibly to this very hour.

"I think we should make a resolution," his new bride had said. Her dark eyes had been glowing with equal parts of promise and provocation. Her lips, rouged and tender from his kisses, had curved into a bewitching smile.

"A resolution?" he'd asked, registering the allure of her expression with every fiber of his being. Echoes of the ecstasy they'd shared a short time before had resonated through him. Blood began to pool and pulse in the flesh between his legs. He'd wanted her again. And again.

"To live happily ever after."

He'd smiled back at Lucy at that point, achingly aware of the throbbing heaviness in his loins. He'd seen her nostrils flare, as though she'd scented his renewed arousal. She'd flushed. He'd known that if he eased down the sheet she had draped around her, he'd find the petal-pink satin of her nipples pebbled and their budding peaks tight and hard.

He'd also known that if he slipped a hand between her thighs, he'd discover a luscious welcome.

"Together."

"Abso—" she'd hiccuped "—lutely."

Chris opened his eyes.

To live happily ever after.

Lord.

He'd had little idea of what those words signified when his wife uttered them on their wedding night. He'd had even less understanding of how to go about translating them into an enduring reality. But somewhere in the back of his mind—and this was one of those dig-down-into-the-gut truths he hadn't grasped until years after his divorce—he'd latched on to the belief that Lucy did. Without perceiving what he was doing, he'd shifted the emotional burden of their marital relationship to her. *She* was to be the keeper of true love's flame. While he . . .

Chris grimaced. He wasn't certain how he'd defined his role in their marriage but he was damned sure that it hadn't corresponded with Lucy's expectations. Damned sure *now,* that is. He'd been clueless back then. He'd botched things up without realizing it, then compounded his unwitting mistakes and sins of omission by trying to pin the blame on his essentially innocent wife.

It had taken him a long time to face up to the responsibility he bore for what had happened. It wasn't that he was a shirker. God, no. The Banks family code didn't allow for that. He simply hadn't understood what he'd done.

He'd heard women talk about men who didn't "get it." Well, except for a few incandescently fine interludes, he'd been such a man when he was with Lucy. If the ugly truth be told, he'd been such a man for quite a while without her, too.

In the immediate aftermath of their breakup, he'd allowed himself to be semibrainwashed by the oh-so-sympathetic postmortems of his relatives and friends. Even after he purged himself of the influence of their insidiously pernicious comments about Lucy's alleged failure to "fit in" to "his"—and their—world, he'd clung to the conviction that he'd been driven to do what he did ten days before their first anniversary.

Yes, his actions had been wrong, he'd acknowledged to himself. But what other choice had he had? He'd been trying to save their marriage, not sink it! If Lucy had stood her ground, as he'd anticipated she'd do, instead of running home to her father, her brothers, et cetera, et cetera and so forth, they might have been able to work things out.

Chris winced inwardly as he remembered the shattered look he'd seen on Lucy's face when she walked into his law office and found him embracing another woman. A woman who, in many ways, was her antithesis. A woman with whom—by most rational standards—he had a great deal in common.

He should have realized the instant he saw Lucy's expression what a hideous misjudgment he'd made, and he should have gone down on his knees to beg her forgiveness. But he'd been too blinded by injured pride and stupidity to comprehend what was going on before his very eyes.

He'd gone after his wife . . . eventually. But by that time, the Falco males had closed ranks against him. And instead of trying to find a way through, around, over or under the familial phalanx they'd established, he'd angrily decided that Lucy's seeming dependence on their protection was conclusive proof that she'd chosen them over him.

She'd filed for divorce. He hadn't contested it. He'd told himself that he no longer gave a damn.

Except he did.

Still did, in point of fact. He cared so much he hurt with it.

Chris took another deep breath. Expelled it in another consciously controlled exhalation. Finally he said, "They would have let you go, you know."

He heard Lucy huff. Felt her toss her head. Her hair tickled the nape of his neck, sending a series of quicksilver tingles cascading down his spine.

"Good for them," she responded, in a tone that communicated precisely the opposite.

No one in his life had ever been able to make him so furious so fast. He was tinder. She was matches. A couple of words, and *whoosh*. A conflagration of temper.

"Dammit, Lucy—"

"I got you into this, Chris," she said, cutting in fiercely. "I'm here for the duration. Deal with it."

His anger dissipated in a rush of bewilderment. He opened and shut his mouth several times, not quite believing he'd heard what he thought he'd heard.

"You got me into this?" he repeated incredulously, mentally cursing his inability to see her expression. Although Lucy unquestionably had acquired a great deal of polish during the past decade, their conversation in the hotel bar had given him ample opportunity to discern that she was still prone to wearing her emotions on her face. "How in heaven's name do you figure that?"

"I knew there was something strange about the security guard, and I didn't do anything about it. I didn't take the time to check the credentials of those two supposed repairmen, either, and I should have." The words came in a rush, like floodwaters through a just-breached dam. She'd obviously given the matter a lot of thought. "Because I wanted to impress you with my job and how great I am at it, I put on this big song and dance about needing to go back to the office to pick up my files. The truth is, there's nothing in them that couldn't have waited until next week. I also gave in to the idea of sharing a taxi with you. If I was going to come back here at all, I should have come back alone! Then I let myself be caught off guard by Tom and Dick Spivey. And because you were here—where you wouldn't have been, if it hadn't been for me—you raced to my rescue and nearly got your brains bashed in by an ex-convict named Percival Johnson!''

Chris blinked, slightly overwhelmed by this impassioned recitation. Yet, as absurd as his ex-wife's self-castigating assertions were, he wasn't really surprised that she'd made them. Lucia Annette Falco had always been quick to hold herself responsible when things went wrong. Quicker still to try to fix them.

He was on the verge of doing something beyond stupid—like inquiring when she was going to get around to blaming herself for the hole in the ozone layer or the lack of civility in American political discourse—when his brain replayed a fragment of what she'd said.

Because I wanted to impress you . . .

Chris was jolted by an emotion he couldn't—or was it wouldn't?—put a name to.

"Why would you want to impress me, Lucy?" His voice was tight. So was his throat. There was a constriction in his chest, too, and it had nothing to do with the physical ties that bound him to his ex-wife.

"Wh-what?"

"You said you put on a big song and dance about needing to come back here and pick up your files because you wanted to impress me. Those ten years and that divorce decree are still between us. Why should my opinion matter to you?"

No answer.

"Lucy?"

"Why do you think?"

"I don't know." He wasn't going to let her stonewall. "That's the reason I'm asking."

Lucy started to tremble. Her breathing pattern frayed.

Tell me, he urged silently. *Whatever it is. Tell me.*

"I didn't mean to say it," she whispered after nearly a minute.

"Obviously. But you did."

"Leave it alone, Chris. Please."

"I can't."

"Won't, you mean."

"Lucy—"

"I did it because I wanted you to know how much I've changed!" she burst out without warning. *"Because I wanted you to understand I'm not some blue-collar bimbo anymore!"*

There was an awful silence.

Chris swallowed convulsively, stunned right down to his socks. Dear Lord, he thought. He'd asked for it, and she'd hauled off and given it to him. The implications of the words she'd flung at him were shaming. Did she really, truly believe he'd perceived her in the way she'd suggested? Was that the impression he'd left with her?

"Lucy..." he began very carefully, feeling as though the words he was about to utter were razor-sharp and had the potential to slice his throat open. "I knew you'd changed the moment we bumped into each other."

"My hair." Her voice was bitter.

"No!" He clenched his hands, wondering if he was going to end up adding that impulsive comment to the list of things he would regret till the day he died. "Okay. Okay. Yes. Yes, I noticed you'd cut your hair, and I blurted it out. I tried to explain why I did that. But if you think I thought— If you think I *think*— God, Lucy! Give me a little credit. Or, if you can't manage that, give yourself some. Heaven knows, you deserve it. You were all potential the first time we met. Now you exude accomplishment. Achievement. I recognized that long before you did your routine about the files. I looked into your eyes tonight and I saw it. I listened to you speak and I heard it in every word that came out of your mouth. As for the other..." He broke off, inhaling sharply, trying to rein in his runaway emotions. "Yes, your background is different from mine. And yes, I was aware of that difference during our relationship. But I never... *ever*... considered you a bimbo."

"So I just imagined you ogling my boobs that first night you came into my family's restaurant?"

Chris cursed under his breath. He'd admitted to and apologized for that ungentlemanly behavior shortly after he introduced himself to Lucy. She'd subsequently teased him about it, seeming to relish his susceptibility to her feminine charms. Had that playfulness been a front?

"What do you want me to say, Lucy?" he asked rawly. "You have a gorgeous body. I noticed it eleven and a half years ago. I noticed it again tonight. I couldn't help it. If truth be told, I'm not sure I'd want to help it if somebody gave me the option! I'm not blind. I'm not a eunuch. I'm not *dead!* But my checking out your chest doesn't mean I don't know you've got a hell of a lot more going for you than a beautiful pair of breasts! And just for the record, the first thing I noticed about you that night in Falco's Pizzeria was your smile. It had me hooked hard and deep long before I started fantasizing about what was under that little white T-shirt you had on."

There was no response from his ex-wife. No sound. No movement.

Chris strained against his bonds. It was a futile effort.

Still no response.

He licked his lips, feeling a bead of sweat course down his spine.

"Lucy?"

"You...you never said anything like that before, Chris." It was impossible to get a fix on her tone. Despite her proximity, her voice seemed to be traveling across a great distance to reach him.

"I thought you knew," he answered, then reconsidered. "No," he amended with a small shake of his head, realizing he'd been less than honest. "I *assumed* you knew. I never really thought about it when we were together."

"But you've thought about it since?"

"Oh...yeah." He left it at that. He doubted he had the words—or was it the nerve?—to go any farther at this particular moment.

"While you were *visualizing* me?" A hint of wryness crept into her voice. Chris suspected the infusion of it was deliberate. He had the feeling that Lucy wasn't ready to go any farther with this line of discussion, either.

"Well—"

The door to the storage room opened. Torn between relief and resentment, Chris turned his head. Dick Spivey— previously Tom the security guard—stepped in, sans his plumed and spangled mask.

"Oh, this is good," he announced approvingly, rubbing his palms together. "This is *very* good."

Although he was far from being certain he wanted to know the answer, Chris felt he needed to ask. "What's good?"

"You two. Talking to each other." Dick beamed. "I heard you through the door."

"You were *eavesdropping* on us?"

Dick's smile vanished. He shifted his gaze from Chris to Lucy, clearly hurt by the accusatory tone of her question. "You were yelling."

Lucy slumped a little. Chris's fetters tightened as a result of her sagging forward. "Oh...God."

"I didn't hear everything." Dick tugged at the collar of his uniform, his scraggly mustache twitching. "You don't have to be embarrassed, okay? It's very important for married people to—"

"Chris and I are *not* married! That's *not*, Dick. *N-O-T*. As in, we got a divorce!"

The would-be robber of the mysterious Red Treasure rolled his eyes. "I know that, Lucy. Unlike *some* people I could name, I listen to what people tell me and I remember it."

"Except when it involves locking doors," Chris muttered, recalling an observation Butch Johnson had made.

Dick made a huffy sound and crossed his arms in front of his less-than-impressive chest. "That's a cheap shot," he said sulkily. "Even for a lawyer."

It probably was, Chris acknowledged to himself. Still, it might help alleviate some of the guilt with which Lucy had so unnecessarily lumbered herself if he drove home the truth behind it. And if that happened...

It was ironic. When he got into the cab with Lucy back at the hotel, he'd been praying that something would happen to prolong their time together. A flat tire, maybe. Or a traffic jam. Anything to defer the moment when she'd bid him good-night and walk away.

Well, his prayers had been answered, in a fashion that strongly suggested God had a rather bizarre sense of humor. But he hadn't capitalized on their enforced intimacy. Instead, honor—and a desire to protect—had compelled him to do everything he could think of to bring it to an end.

If only he could get Lucy to cooperate!

"Maybe so, Dick," he replied. "But the fact is, Lucy and I wouldn't be facing the prospect of spending the next day and a half trussed up like turkeys in a dinky room with no windows if we hadn't been able to get into this building. And we wouldn't have been able to get into this building if you'd remembered to lock the front door!"

"No, no, no." Dick shook his head. "Don't you see? You're being negative about this, Chris. You've got to be positive! You've got to regard this as...as...an *opportunity!*"

"An opportunity for what?" Lucy asked. "Psychodrama?"

Dick took a few steps forward and hunkered down beside them. His expression held a mix of solemnity and evangelical fervor.

"Did you two get any marriage counseling before you broke up?" he asked.

Chris stiffened. He felt his ex-wife do the same. He understood why. In the latter days of their marriage, Lucy had broached the possibility of their seeking some kind of help. He'd rejected the idea for several reasons, chief among them being his pigheaded belief that he knew what was "wrong" with their relationship and what she—not he, *she*—had to do to fix it.

"That's none of your business," Lucy said, her diction very precise.

Dick shook his head, plainly undeterred by this unequivocal instruction to butt out. He had the air of a missionary confronting a heathen horde.

"You didn't," he said with a sigh. "I can tell. Well, *I've* had counseling. And based on my experience with Dora-Jean—"

"This is the woman you married and divorced twice?" Chris inserted sardonically, wondering at the fact that Lucy hadn't taken a verbal jab at him.

"Just because we got divorced and redivorced doesn't mean the counseling didn't take," Dick responded serenely. "I learned a lot. Like, you have to open up the lines of communication. Which, yelling or not, you two seemed to be doing before I walked in. But you have to keep 'em humming, you know? Give-and-take. Give-and-take. Back and forth. You have to *share*. That's the key. *Sharing.* Let me start you off. Me and Dora-Jean used to do this all the time. Lucy, why don't you share with Chris—"

The storage room door banged open. Dick started violently, toppling backward and landing heavily on his rump. Tom stomped in.

"Butch wants to know what's takin' you so long," he announced.

"Jeez!" Dick got to his feet, tugging the jacket of his uniform down. "I was having a very important conversation with Chris and Lucy!"

Tom studied him for several seconds, then groaned. "Oh, no. You weren't startin' in with that *share* baloney, were you?"

"It's not baloney!"

"Dora-Jean hated that stuff somethin' fierce, you know."

"I told you not to bad-mouth Dora-Jean!"

"I'm not bad-mouthin' Dora-Jean! But she sure as hell bad-mouthed you and your stupid 'open lines of communication' routine! She said she'd rather sit down on a sharp stick than go through even a teeny-tiny second of that 'sharing' bushwa."

"I don't believe you!"

"Why don't you ask her?"

"Because I don't know where she is!"

"Well, don't look at me," Tom retorted with a contemptuous snort. "I ain't the host of 'Unsolved Mysteries.' Besides, you're the last one who was married to her. It's your job to keep track of her." He turned toward Chris and Lucy. "Dick was *supposed* to come in here and find out what kind of pizza you want."

Chris absorbed this last bit of information with a disturbing degree of equanimity. He wondered what his lack of response said about his mental state.

"You're going out for pizza?" Lucy wanted to know. She, too, seemed only mildly surprised by the idea.

"We're gettin' it delivered," Dick answered, then gave his sibling a baleful look. "'Course we wouldn't have had to bother, if a certain somebody had remembered to bring the groceries I bought like he was *supposed* to do."

"Pizza's better than your old groceries any old day of the week."

"Says who?"

"Says me, and I'm bigger!"

"Yeah, well—"

"I'll eat anything but anchovies," Chris said, in no mood for another round of Spivey squabbling. He twisted, looking back at his ex-wife. "Do you still go for double cheese and pepperoni?"

She twisted around, too. Their gazes connected for a moment. He saw a strange combination of emotions flickering through the depths of her dark eyes. His heart missed a beat. A powerful sense of longing suffused him.

Did you think I'd forget something like that? he wanted to ask. *Oh, Lucy. Lucy! I remember everything about you. And I want you back, sweetheart. I want you back so we can make that happily-ever-after resolution come true.*

"That's fine," she said huskily, then turned away.

"Okeydokey," Dick responded.

"Thirty minutes or less," Tom promised.

The Spiveys trooped out of the storage room, elbowing and shoving each other as they went.

"Lucy—"

The door swung open again. It was Tom.

Chris almost lost it. *"What?"*

The bearded man blinked several times and scratched his chin, then produced a sheepish grin. "Do you have some, uh, money we can borrow so's we can pay for the pizzas?"

Seven

What the former Mr. and Mrs. Christopher Dodson Banks might have chosen to "share" during the thirty minutes that followed was destined to remain a question mark. Barely a second after the storage room door clicked shut behind Tom, a high-pitched drilling sound rent the air. It was soon joined by the heavy thud of a sledgehammer hitting something. The mind-numbing cacophony—punctuated by an occasional crash or curse—was not exactly conducive to meaningful conversation.

The noise ended abruptly, leaving behind what Lucy could only have described as a deafening silence.

"Do you hear that?" she asked Chris, her ears ringing so badly she wasn't able to gauge the volume of her voice.

"What?" her ex-husband practically shouted.

"Nothing!"

"Yeah." He laughed. "Doesn't it sound terrific?"

The storage room door opened a moment later. Butch stepped in. He was covered with flecks of paint and smears of grayish powder. There was a pair of what appeared to be headphones slung around his muscle-corded neck and a vicious-looking knife in his right hand.

Lucy felt herself pale. She also felt Chris go rigid.

"Oh, jeez," the balding ex-convict growled, plainly put out by their reaction. "Don't start with that. I'm here to cut you loose, not slit your damned throats."

"Y-you're letting us go?" Lucy tried not to flinch as Butch squatted down and inserted the blade between her wrists.

"No" He sliced through the duct tape. "I'm letting you get up to eat pizza."

The "getting up" part proved to be a tad problematic, at least for her. The portions of her anatomy that hadn't gone numb were badly cramped or inclined to wobble. Chris, apparently less affected by their ordeal, had to help her stand.

"Easy," he said when she tried to take a step forward and ended up staggering against him like a drunk. He gripped her forearms in much the same way he'd gripped them when they ran into each other outside the office building. Only this time, all that separated his fingers from her flesh was a single layer of finely woven wine-colored wool.

She could feel the warmth from those fingers clear down to the marrow of her bones. The temptation to sag and cling was very, very strong.

Lucy looked up at Chris, as she had after their earlier collision, staring searchingly into his compelling face. What she was looking for, she wasn't sure. She wasn't even certain that this was the right place to find it.

She caught a flash of emerald green in the depths of his hazel eyes. Then, by some strange trick of the lighting, she glimpsed a reflection of her own visage. Her stomach fluttered. Her breath caught briefly at the top of her throat, then escaped between her lips in a shaky rush as her mind suddenly replayed part of the remarkable tribute he'd given her before Dick's precipitate reappearance in the storage room.

Give me a little credit, he'd said with untrammeled intensity. *Or if you can't manage that, give yourself some. Heaven knows, you deserve it.*

It wasn't just his words that had been new to her. His tone had been unfamiliar, as well. The only times she'd heard him speak with anything approaching such raw emotionalism had been in bed, in the heat—at the height—of passion. And whether the shattered syllables and inarticulate sounds he'd uttered then could honestly be described as "speaking" was open to debate.

You were all potential the first time we met, he'd gone on. *Now you exude accomplishment. Achievement. I recognized that long before you did your routine about the files.*

Lucy discovered that she'd lifted her newly freed hands and placed them against her ex-husband's chest. She lowered them quickly, the movement causing the outer swell of her breasts to brush against the backs of his thumbs. She felt her nipples begin to stiffen beneath the fabric of her bodice and bra.

Chris's fingers tightened. "Lucy?"

"I'm okay," she managed, trying to ease back. "Thank you for... c-catching me."

"Anytime." He released her, but stayed close. Under normal circumstances, Lucy would have balked at this seeming protectiveness and asserted that she was perfectly capable of standing on her own. But these were not normal circumstances. Besides. Fundamental honesty forced her to acknowledge that the odds of her walking out of the storage room without her former spouse's support were no better than fifty-fifty.

"Pizza's getting cold," Butch informed them gruffly. "You about done dancin' around with each other?"

Lucy felt her cheeks grow warm. She began fussing with her dress, smoothing wrinkles and brushing off bits of lint.

"For the moment." Chris's tone was enviably—and irritatingly—calm. "I don't suppose you have a couple of extra pairs of ear protectors we could use after we finish eating."

Lucy stopped fussing. She shot a questioning look at her ex-husband, then glanced toward their balding captor.

"Now you've gone and disappointed me, Chris," Butch said. "I'd been given to understand that you two were engaged in openin' up your lines of communication. Kind of hard to do that wearing earplugs, don't you think?" He gave a gravelly chuckle. "Dick's gonna be crushed. He was sure you were in here *sharing*."

"Dick will survive. But another half hour of that noise you were making and the only thing Lucy and I will be 'sharing' is permanent damage to our auditory nerves."

Butch looked startled by this acerbic assertion. Then he frowned.

"Damnation!" he exclaimed after a moment, sounding genuinely upset. "I never thought about that. It was pretty bad, huh?"

Lucy felt Chris's gaze flicked toward her. For reasons she couldn't have explained, she took it as a cue. *"What was that?"* she asked loudly, cupping her right ear.

"Okay. Okay." Butch grimaced. "I get the point. Don't worry. The worst is over."

If there'd been a window in the storage room, Lucia Annette Falco would have taken a look outside. Because instinct told her that if the worst of this mess was over, there'd be pigs in the sky... flying.

They dined in a circle, sitting on the floor. Lucy and Chris were side by side. The erstwhile robbers of the Red Treasure sat opposite them, blocking quick access to the door that opened into the hallway.

"Somethin' wrong with your pizza, Lucy?" Tom Spivey asked, through a partially masticated blob of underbaked crust, gloppy mozzarella and watery tomato sauce, about twenty minutes into their meal.

"I'm just not very hungry." Suppressing a small shudder of distaste, she set aside the pepperoni-studded slice she'd been nibbling at. She kept her eyes lowered, not wanting to look at the damage that had been done to Gulliver's Travels' main—and recently redecorated—work area.

She'd seen more than enough when she walked out of the storage room. Every surface in the place had been dusted with what appeared to be a mixture of pulverized paint, plaster and cement. And that X-marked spot she'd wondered about? Well, that had been obliterated. So, too, had the portion of wall it had appeared on.

"Lucy's accustomed to a higher quality of food than this," Chris commented, taking a swig of soda. He'd been right behind Lucy when she stepped into the work area and registered the mess. She'd felt him place a hand on her shoulder. The touch had conveyed a wordless message of both sympathy and support.

"How's that?" Butch wanted to know.

"Her family runs one of the best pizza places in Chicago."

"*The* best," Lucy corrected automatically as she picked up a can of soda.

"*The* best." Chris matched her inflection perfectly. "That's where we met."

"You're both from Chicago, huh?" The query came from Dick. Although he had made only a few comments during the meal thus far, Lucy was uneasily aware that he'd been scrutinizing her and Chris with a peculiarly expectant expression.

"That's right."

Tom took another huge bite of pizza, then asked, "So how come you're here?"

"*Duh,*" Dick responded sarcastically. "This is where Lucy works!"

"Umph." Tom chewed several times, then gulped. "Yeah. Right."

"What about you, Harvard?" Butch inquired. "What are you doing in our fair Peach State?"

"Duh-huh." It was Tom. "He's bein' with Lucy!"

Lucy's pulse jumped. Her fingers spasmed against the soda can she'd been sipping from, denting the condensation-hazed aluminium.

"Chris is *not* with me," she disputed, trying to ignore a sudden, treacherous warmth between her thighs. She told herself she was tired. Upset. Vulnerable. Still shaken by some of the things Chris had said to her in the storage room. Her physical responses were suspect in the extreme. They were no indication of how she really felt. What she truly wanted.

"Yeah, he is," the bearded Spivey brother argued. "And you're with him. I mean, you even said!"

"I did not—"

"Uh-huh, you did. When you yelled about not letting us let you go. You said you were gonna stay here *with him.*"

Lucy looked at Chris. He looked back, his expression enigmatic to the point of being unreadable. Her pulse jumped a second time. After several shaky moments, she tore her gaze from his and turned toward Tom, saying, "I didn't mean it that way."

"Sounded like you did."

"Look." She leaned forward, wanting to make certain everyone understood the situation. Including her. "Chris flew into Atlanta from New York for a job interview, and he couldn't fly back because of bad weather. We just happened to run into each other."

"Fate," Dick stated smugly.

"An *accident.*"

"Lucy—" It was Chris. His quiet invocation of her name was accompanied by a touch to her upper arm. She jerked away, appalled by the electrified tingling the brief contact set off.

"What happened between the time you ran into each other and the time you came back here?" Butch wanted to know.

"Nothing!"

"We had one drink. No strings attached. Lucy picked up the tab."

There was a long pause. Lucy spent it staring at the floor, trying to get a grip on herself.

"You must be a real good cook, huh, Lucy," Tom suddenly remarked. His tone suggested he'd been giving the matter considerable thought.

Lucy started and brought her head up, thrown by this seeming non sequitur. "Excuse...me?"

"You must be a real good cook." Tom paused, fishing a morsel of sausage out of his beard and popping it in his mouth. "With your family havin' a restaurant and all."

Lucy glanced toward Chris once again. She didn't even think about it. She just did it. But somewhere in the back of her mind, she was uneasily aware that she was reverting to a habit formed during their courtship.

This time, her ex-husband's expression was very easy to decipher. He looked amused. And no wonder. Aside from an uncanny knack for being able to judge the exact instant when a boiling pot of pasta was about to achieve the perfect stage of al dente doneness, she was a washout in the kitchen.

"Actually, Lucy was more involved in the business side of Falco's Pizzeria," Chris said smoothly. He held her gaze a heady half second longer than was strictly necessary, then turned his attention toward Tom, Dick and Butch. "She worked out front all through high school. Pretty much a full-time job, but she still graduated with high honors. Same thing while she was in college. Which she attended on a National Merit Scholarship."

"Wow." Tom contemplated Lucy with something akin to awe. "I didn't even graduate eighth grade. I kind of flunked attendance."

"I dropped out of high school," Butch confessed, then muffled a carbonation-induced belch. "But I got my GED in prison."

"I learned security guarding through one of those courses you see on TV," Dick volunteered. "Dora-Jean enrolled me."

Caught up in trying to stem the rush of pleasure she'd felt at her ex-husband's very complimentary condensation of her educational record, Lucy almost missed the significance of the next to last sentence. Then the phrase *security guarding* clicked in her brain.

"Wait a minute!" she exclaimed, swatting back an errant lock of hair. "You actually *are* a security guard?"

Dick looked offended. "I told you I was!"

"A person can get in really bad trouble, pretendin' to be a security guard," Tom pointed out.

Brown eyes met hazel ones once again. Almost before her gaze connected with his, Lucy knew that Chris had had exactly the same reaction to the previous comment as she. Namely, that the "really bad trouble" one could get into for impersonating a security guard was nothing compared to the penalties one might incur for committing crimes such as, oh, say, breaking and entering, felonious assault, kidnapping and grand theft.

I know it's tempting, she could practically hear Chris saying inside her head. *But maybe we should refrain from reminding them that this caper could land them in prison until the middle of the next century if they're caught.*

Lucy drew a shaky breath. She'd tried to forget what they were like, these moments of unspoken communion. She'd experienced them frequently with Chris during their courtship and the early months of their marriage. But near the end of their relationship—

She shoved the past away again, painfully conscious that this was getting harder and harder to do. Then she turned back to Dick and said, "So the things you told me about

Ray Price—about your subbing for him—those were true, too?''

"Of course they were true." Dick's mouth twitched. His mustache wriggled. "What did you think, Lucy? That I tied him up and stashed him someplace?''

Butch nearly choked on the gulp of soda he'd just taken. "Now where would she get an idea like *that*, I wonder?''

Dick glared at him. "Just because I had to do it to her and Chris doesn't mean I'm gonna *plan* to do it to somebody else! That'd be...uh...uh...uh...''

"Premeditation?" Chris offered.

"Yeah!" Dick nodded his head. "Premeditation! And that's even worse than pretending to be a security guard!''

"But don't you have to premeditate if you're gonna do that, Dick?" Tom asked, crumpling a soda can like a piece of tissue paper. He seemed absolutely serious about his question. "I mean, you gotta premeditate to get the right uniform—''

"Of all the *stupid*—''

"Speaking of premeditation," Chris said, cutting off both the Spiveys. "I imagine you must have done a considerable amount of advance planning for this, ah...job.''

"And I imagine you imagine maybe we should've done a little more?" Butch countered.

There was an odd edge to his voice. It took Lucy a moment to realize that the edge was embarrassment. She felt a prickle of uneasiness as she noted the rigidity of Percival Johnson's posture. It was her experience that an embarrassed male was a potentially dangerous one. She glanced toward her ex-husband.

"I didn't say that, Butch," Chris replied, sustaining the balding convict's gaze for several unwavering seconds. That he could have forced the other man to look away, Lucy didn't doubt for a second. But he chose to disengage first.

It was not how a Falco male would have handled the situation, she reflected with a curious pang. Dollars to doughnuts, her male relatives would have provoked a fight.

Lucy liked Chris's tactics better. Much better.

"You didn't have to, Harvard," Butch returned after a beat, the tension easing out of his back and shoulders. "It's true."

"We *planned,* Butch!" Tom protested. "We planned lots!" He shifted toward Chris and Lucy and explained, "Butch and me started casin' places to hit right after Dick got his job with the guard company. We had a couple of choices. Then stuff kind of clicked for us. We started hearin' about this Red Treasure. Dick found out he was gonna be guardin' here over New Year's. All that."

Lucy looked at Dick. "So, you went to work for the security company, uh..." She searched for an alternative to the word *planning.* "...figuring you were going to pull some kind of uh..." She paused again, finally recalling the non-pejorative noun her ex-husband had used earlier. "...uh, job?"

"Oh, no." Dick shook his head to make this crystal-clear. "I was looking forward to an exciting career in private-sector law enforcement."

"Then Dora-Jean dumped him again because of all that *sharing* stuff, and he decided—"

"*Dora-Jean did not—*"

"Shut up!" Butch ordered sharply. "Both of you, just shut up!"

The Spiveys subsided into grumpy silence. Lucy traded looks with Chris.

"Butch," she said after a moment or two.

"Yeah?"

"If it isn't too personal... what did you do to get sent to prison?"

Tom snickered. Butch gave him a glare that could have peeled paint at fifty paces. Tom suddenly got very busy stuffing his mouth with cold, greasy pizza. Butch turned back to Lucy, his expression turning sheepish.

"I got sent to prison because I made a dumb-cluck move during a burglary," he said. "I got into the house fine, or so

I thought. Nobody was home. There was a ton of stuff to steal, including this video-game hookup. Really expensive deal. Top-of-the-line. I go for that sort of thing, you know? Anyway, I turned it on and all of a sudden the television lit up like World War III." He gestured with great animation, sketching an impression of what had appeared on the screen. For one weird moment, Lucy found herself thinking of Wayne Dweck. "I mean, there was bullets flyin', bombs burstin' and body parts all over the place. Best damned effects I'd ever seen. So, I grabbed the control and started to play."

"And he was *still* playin' when the cops showed up because of the silent alarm he didn't know he tripped," Tom concluded in a rush. "He didn't even know they were there until one of the cops kind of tapped him on the shoulder."

There was a volatile silence. Lucy edged toward Chris, fearing Tom had finally gone too far. She felt her ex-husband stiffen, and knew that he was contemplating the same possibility.

"Tom?" The question was soft. Almost gentle.

"Yeah, Butch?" The response was wary.

"Do you remember earlier, when Chris and Lucy were talking about short-term memory loss?"

"Uh . . . no."

"Well, I'm of the opinion that you have a serious case of it."

"Think he remembers what *he* did to get put in prison?" Dick asked snidely.

"Oh, God," Lucy heard Chris mutter. "Here we go again."

"It wasn't somethin' *wrong!*" Tom cried, thumping his hands against the floor.

"He stole a police car," Butch informed Chris and Lucy.

Tom was almost beside himself. "Yeah, but, that's not why I got put in prison!"

Lucy darted a glance at Chris. He lifted his eyebrows, clearly inquiring whether she was absolutely sure she wanted to get in the middle of this. She felt the corners of her mouth curl in an admission that yes, she was. He smiled knowingly and nodded his head, prompting her to get on with it.

"Why did you get put in prison, Tom?" she asked.

"I don't have to tell. I'm takin' that amendment thing against self-discrimination."

"You have to be under oath to do that, Tom," Chris advised him mildly.

"Really?"

"Really. Sorry."

"Well, *that's* stupid."

"No, that's the Constitution."

"Come on, just spit it out," Butch prodded. "You're in court, sitting next to your lawyer. The cop whose car you stole..."

"Borrowed."

"...*stole* and crashed into a telephone pole..."

"I didn't mean for that to happen! I get the brake and the gas mixed up sometimes!"

"Well, maybe if you got your *license*—"

"Shut up, Dick," Butch snapped. "Let Tom finish his story. Okay, Tom. The cop's on the stand, and the D.A. asks him if the guy who took his vehicle is in the courtroom. And you—" he made a prompting gesture "—what?"

Tom looked down and muttered something into his beard.

"I don't think Chris and Lucy heard that."

"It's all right, Tom," Lucy said quickly, assailed by a pang of pity. "We don't really need to know."

Tom heaved a great sigh and looked up. "No. That's okay. I'll tell you. When the lawyer asked was the man who took the police car in the court, I raised my hand and said, 'Yeah, I'm sittin' right here.'"

Chris and Lucy were returned to storage room captivity a few minutes later. Before they were, Lucy checked her watch. She gasped when she saw the time, then looked up at her ex-husband.

"Happy New Year," he said ironically.

Butch reached into his filthy jumpsuit and pulled out a pocket watch. "I've got one-oh-eight," he announced.

"One-oh-eight . . . and twelve seconds," Dick concurred, consulting his wristwatch.

"Nine-fifteen," Tom chipperly declared, glancing at his own timepiece.

"*Nine-fifteen?* We were supposed to synchronize our watches, you jerk!"

"I did. But I think Lucy hit mine when she was fightin' us, and it stopped."

Eight

Chris shifted, trying to find a comfortable position. Even a semicomfortable position. Heck, he'd settle for *any* position in which he didn't feel in imminent danger of having his spinal cord punctured by a piece of metal.

In honor of their passage from the old year to the new, Butch and the Spivey boys had relented a bit on the tying-up situation. While they'd insisted that both he and Lucy had to be fettered, they'd agreed to deep-six the duct-tape restraints around the wrists and ankles. They'd also given in on the back-to-back issue. He and his ex-wife were now securely attached to floor-to-ceiling shelf supports on opposite sides of the storage room.

Chris had expected that being face-to-face would make it easier for him and Lucy to talk. It hadn't worked out that way. A curious kind of constraint had settled over both of them as soon as their captors exited. They'd exchanged a few desultory comments, then fallen silent. The longer this silence had gone on, the worse the tension in the small storage room had become. It had finally reached the point where Lucy had stopped *looking* at him!

He shifted again, noticing for the first time that there was a tear in one of his trouser legs. Oh, well, he thought with a mental shrug. It wasn't as though this were the only navy blue suit he owned.

He glanced across at Lucy. She was sitting motionless, her shapely legs outstretched and crossed neatly at the ankles. Although the figure-skimming dress she had on appeared to be intact, the stockings that clung to her lower limbs had multiple runs.

Her head was slightly tilted back, and her eyes were closed. The rise and fall of her breasts was slow and steady.

She wasn't sleeping. She obviously wanted him to think she was, but he knew she wasn't. He could read tension in every line of her curvaceous body. Lucy, asleep, was as bonelessly relaxed as a rag doll.

Or so he very vividly remembered.

Chris shifted a third time, doing his best to ignore a sudden stirring in his groin. He cleared his throat. Lucy continued to play possum.

"I'd forgotten what a soft touch you are, Lucia Annette," he finally ventured, although he'd done nothing of the kind.

He'd experienced a great many conflicting emotions about Lucy's one-on-one approach to compassion during their marriage, including a bitter resentment of the fact that the time she expended on other people was time she didn't have for him. But in an odd way, she'd set him on the professional course that had led to his being offered the foundation job that had brought him to Atlanta.

The memory of her willingness to reach out and help troubled people as best she could had prompted him to start doing *pro bono* work for a free legal clinic in one of New York's poorer neighborhoods. While he wouldn't deny that he relished the high-powered cut and thrust of corporate work—he liked winning, and he liked winning big—the cases he handled for the clinic nourished a part of his soul he hadn't known was hungry.

Lucy didn't rise to his verbal bait immediately. Indeed, he could sense her debating whether to ignore it altogether. Finally, she lifted her eyelids a fraction of an inch and peered down her nose at him. After a few moments of this, she opened her eyes completely and brought her head down to a normal angle.

"What's that supposed to mean?" she asked, adjusting her position a bit. He wondered fleetingly whether she missed the feel of his back pressing against hers as he missed the feel of hers pressing against his. That their being roped together had been uncomfortable went without saying. Yet there'd been something...reassuring...about the contact.

"You. Just a little while ago. Telling Tom it really wasn't necessary for him to say what he'd done to get himself thrown in the slammer. And you tried to let all three of our, ah, 'hosts' off the hook before that, too. Remember? You changed the subject right after Butch admitted they don't know what this Red Treasure thing is. You didn't want to rub their noses in how clueless they are."

She cocked an eyebrow, a hint of pugnacity entering her expression. "And I suppose you do?"

"I think I have a little less compunction about it than you do. It didn't bother me for a nanosecond when I tricked Dick into spilling part of the beans about this idiotic heist of theirs."

"Maybe not. Then again, you had a perfect chance to humiliate Butch, and you let it slide."

Chris blinked, caught off guard by this assertion. He hadn't realized that Lucy was watching his exchange with Percival Johnson so closely. And even if he had, he wouldn't have expected her to respond to it so...well, he was tempted to say so positively, but he didn't want to press his luck.

"Guy-style psych-out." He shrugged. "You've probably seen your brothers and cousins do it hundreds of times."

"Your 'guy-style' isn't the same as their 'guy-style,' Chris."

Ten years ago, he would have assumed that the corollary to this wry statement was that his then-wife preferred her relatives' brand of masculine behavior to his own. He wasn't ready to assume anything now.

He sucked in a lungful of air, wrestling with some hard truths. He wanted Lucy's approval. And her admiration. But above all, he wanted her forgiveness for what he'd done to her. To them. Because if she could find it in her generous heart to forgive, there might...*just might*...be a chance for them to begin again.

A slightly bizarre realization slid from the shadowy edges of his consciousness to the forefront of his brain. God Almighty, he thought. If he managed to achieve a reconciliation with his ex-wife, at least some of the credit for it would have to go to Butch and the Spivey brothers. And knowing Lucy, she'd want to find a way to repay the debt. She'd probably want to testify on their behalf when—definitely when, not if—the trio was captured and brought to trial. Heck. She'd probably lobby him to defend the idiots!

Chris felt his lips twist. What was it Dick had said? Something about regarding this situation as an opportunity?

The sound of Lucy sighing refocused his awareness.

"What is it?" he asked.

"Maybe I *am* a soft touch." The concession was rueful. "They're criminals, for heaven's sake! Two of them have done jail time. One of them clobbered you over the head. They've also wrecked all the beautiful redecoration work Abby Davis did...."

"But?" he prompted, as her litany of charges trailed off into silence.

Her gaze met his. "What can I say? I feel sorry for them. I mean, they seem so...so..."

"Stupid?"

Lucy tried to look shocked. She sustained the illusion for about two and a half seconds, then broke up. "That sounds so..." She gave a gurgle of laughter. "...*judgmental.*"

"I was only quoting them on each other."

"I don't remember anyone calling *Butch* stupid."

Chris feigned a frown, pretending to think back. "You know," he said after a few moments, "I think you're right."

"I'm not saying it isn't a valid description, you understand. At least, not as far as poor Tom and Dick are concerned. Still, it's not a very nice word."

"Okay. How about..." He cocked his head, searching for an appropriate euphemism. "...mentally challenged?"

"Intellectually deprived," she countered instantly, her brown eyes sparkling. The makeup she'd used to enhance them had smudged a bit, adding a sultry hint of heaviness to her lids.

"Half-armed in any war of wits?"

"Ooh... That's really nasty." A dimple-displaying smile deprived the comment of any sting. Then Lucy grew reflective, worrying her lower lip with the edge of her upper front teeth. Whatever gloss or coloring she'd been wearing on her mouth had long since worn off. "I wonder if there's some sort of course in remedial criminality they could take."

"Forget nasty. Now you're talking downright scary."

"I suppose a little knowledge *would* be a dangerous thing in the case of the Spivey brothers...."

There was a pause. Chris adjusted his position anew. He had to be careful how he moved his head. If he tilted it back too far, something jabbed against the egg-size lump he'd received from Butch.

The lighthearted atmosphere engendered by their rapid-fire bantering about their captors leaked away. The pause consolidated into another uncomfortable silence.

Chris knew that it was his move. His...*opportunity.* He also understood that there were certain subjects that were taboo until Lucy chose to broach them. Chief among these was the night she'd walked into his office and found him kissing his onetime girlfriend, Irene Houghton.

Until Lucy clearly signaled that she wanted to talk about that episode...

That she was *ready* to talk about it...

He took a slow, steadying breath. There were other issues that were not off-limits, he told himself. Issues that it was up to him to raise and resolve.

"Lucy?"

"Mmm?"

"Was I really such a...snob...when we were together?"

Her gaze slammed into his. He watched a wave of color storm up her throat and into her face. She flushed to the roots of her tousled brown hair. Then the surge of hot blood reversed itself. It drained away, leaving her very pale. Violet-gray shadows showed starkly beneath her eyes, like dirty thumbprints on a sheet of ivory-colored vellum.

"I never said you were a snob, Chris."

"Not in so many words," he conceded, holding her eyes. "But you did think—maybe you *still* think—that I used to believe you were a blue-collar bimbo. And if that doesn't imply snobbery on my part, I don't know what would. You also seemed stunned when I told Tom, Dick and Butch about Falco's Pizzeria and all the rest."

"Not...stunned."

"Surprised, then."

A strange series of emotions flickered across Lucy's features. "You said yourself, my background is different than yours."

"Yes, I did. And yes, it is. But *different* isn't a code word for *inferior*. Not to me. Especially not where you're concerned. And whatever I did during the time we were together to make you think that it was..." He broke off, shaking his head. His throat was tight and dry. Finally he resumed. "I'm sorry, Lucy. From the bottom of my heart, for whatever it was...*I am sorry.*"

His ex-wife bit her lower lip and blinked several times in rapid succession. Then she looked down, staring fixedly at her lap. After ten, maybe fifteen seconds, of silence, she said, "I know I wasn't the kind of woman your family and friends expected you to marry."

Chris didn't deny it. How could he? For better or worse—and the scales seemed to be tilting toward the latter at the moment—it was true.

"I had the distinct impression that your hooking up with me shocked the hell out of most of your friends and relatives, too," he countered bluntly.

Lucy's head came up. Her dark eyes were glistening. A splotch of reddish-pink had blossomed on each of her cheeks.

"So?" Her voice was raw. "No matter how they reacted in the beginning, they all ended up liking you. You won them over to your side. Even my oldest brother, Vinnie. They thought you were terrific until . . . until . . ."

Chris waited, muscles clenched, gut knotted.

Lucy made an inarticulate sound and looked away. Her mouth was trembling, and her breath was coming in quick, shallow bursts.

"They opened their arms to me," Chris finally acknowledged, telling himself to be patient. The debacle he'd precipitated ten nights before their first wedding anniversary hadn't just happened. It had been the culmination of months of mistakes and misunderstandings. The former had to be corrected and the latter clarified before there would be a prayer of undoing the real damage. "Not right away. Why should they have? Your father, brothers, uncles, cousins—all of your friends—knew how special you were. They needed to be sure the man you'd agreed to marry wasn't totally unworthy of you. But whatever reservations they had, every single one of them made me feel welcome on our wedding day. I became a Falco as much as you became a Banks. Probably more so, in their eyes."

Lucy gave a jerky little nod, her throat working.

"But you didn't get the same treatment from my side of the aisle, did you?" The words were bitter on his tongue. "And to make things worse, I didn't see it. I didn't... realize."

She brought her eyes back to his. "I tried to fit in, Chris. To do what was... expected. Your m-mother..."

"Oh, yes. My mother. I can imagine."

Although his mother had been her coolly polite self during his marriage, she'd turned viciously critical about Lucy after the breakup. But the harshness of her comments had ended up boomeranging. The portrait she'd attempted to paint of her ex-daughter-in-law simply had not jibed with the woman Chris knew in his head and heart, his gut and groin. For every negative thing she'd said, a small voice deep within him had offered a contradiction. Her intent had been to make him say good riddance to his ex-wife. What she'd done instead was to drive him to the point where all he could think was *Dear Lord, what have I done?*

"Elizabeth tried to help me," Lucy asserted. "She gave me advice. Pointed out when I made mistakes. She wanted me to be... good... enough for you."

"*Good* enough for me? God, Lucy. You were much better than I deserved!"

"You didn't think that in the beginning."

"I fell for you like a ton of bricks the first time I laid eyes on you."

"But you weren't sure about us."

Chris caught his breath, finally realizing what she must mean. Those weeks he'd spent trying to analyze his attraction to her—

"I wasn't sure about *me*, Lucy!" he burst out. "Not about you."

"I don't... understand."

He took a few seconds to marshal his explanation. He wanted to get the words right. To make the truth of the matter very, very clear.

"You used to joke a lot about the burden of being the only female Falco of your generation," he began. "Well, I'm the only male Banks of mine. Which is—*was*—no laughing matter. I was brought up knowing that there were a great many things I was expected to do, and do superlatively. I was also taught there were lines I shouldn't cross and ideas I shouldn't challenge, because that wasn't the Banks family way. I pretty much went along with the program for twenty-four years. Then...*pow.* I walked into a pizza place I'd never heard of to meet an old college buddy who ended up pulling a no-show and I saw you. King Kong doing a swan dive off the Empire State Building didn't go down harder than I did. But what I felt toward you was so...*different*...from anything I'd ever felt, I had to question it. I started to worry that maybe I was going through some delayed form of adolescent rebellion. That I was using you to break out of the Banks mold." He swallowed, remembering. "The possibility made me a little sick. Maybe even a little crazy. So I held back. I didn't want to hurt you."

There was a long silence. Chris watched Lucy, painfully aware of the ugly irony attached to his last sentence. He hadn't wanted to hurt her. Yet he had. Unintentionally at first, yes. But the pain he'd inflicted when he arranged for her to walk in on him and Irene Houghton...

God help him. That had been deliberate.

"I never told you what my very first response to you was, did I?" Lucy finally asked. Her voice sounded strained. Her pallor had increased.

Chris gave a humorless laugh. "You were ticked off because I was eyeballing your chest."

"It was more than that." She gnawed her lower lip. Her eyes seemed unfocused, as though she were reliving the reaction she was about to describe. "In that second or two before you looked up and our eyes met, I decided you were some kind of stuck-up rich guy who was as out of place in my family's restaurant as...as... Oh, Lord. I don't know, exactly! Caviar on a cannoli, maybe. But I resented you, Chris. And I—I *envied* you. I was standing there sweating like a pig and worrying about how I was going to make up the difference between the scholarship money I'd won and another two semesters of college tuition and you came strolling in all cool and calm and classy, sporting a haircut that probably cost you fifty or sixty bucks...."

"Lucy." He was appalled. "Oh, Lucy."

"It's taken me a long time to face up to this," she went on doggedly. "Because I turned it all around. That thing I practically screamed at you earlier? About wanting you to know that I'm not a blue-collar bimbo anymore? Well, deep in my heart, I knew you never thought I was. Maybe your parents did. And still do. Maybe your friends, too, although some of them were genuinely nice to me while we were together. But when I dig down to the bottom line, I know the main person who believed I was a blue-collar bimbo was *me*. *Different* might not have been a code word for *inferior* to you, but it was to me. Only I couldn't admit to that. I'd spent my whole life telling the world how proud I was of who I was and what I was. So I twisted things to fit my perceptions. *I* wasn't the one who wanted to make me over into the perfect Mrs. Christopher Dodson Banks, it was *you*. My insecurities about fitting into what you called 'your side of the aisle' weren't *my* fault. How could they be? Everyone who knew me would tell you I had confidence coming out of my ears! It was *you* who made me feel unsure. And when I saw myself pretending to be someone I wasn't, when I felt my sense of identity slipping away—when it seemed to me that Ms. Stand-Up-for-Herself Falco was turning into a spineless dishrag—*I blamed you.*"

It took Chris nearly a minute to find his voice. The guilt he felt was crushing. He was also humbled by his ex-wife's insistence on exposing what she saw to be her own faults. She had no reason to mitigate his culpability in their marriage.

No reason save that she was a woman of implacable personal integrity, as well as hard-earned professional accomplishment.

"I never knew," he finally said, cringing inwardly at the inadequacy of the admission.

She looked him square in the eyes for several seconds, then averted her gaze. "I never said."

"Oh, Lucy." Chris shook his head, regret searing through him like acid. "You shouldn't have had to."

From outside the storage room door came the sound of hammering.

Ask him, Lucy prodded herself. *Yes, it'll be ten years and a divorce decree late. But ask him!*

She couldn't.

Not yet.

The question was fully formed. It had been fully formed for a long, long time. But she couldn't force it out.

If she asked and Chris answered yes, it would break her heart. She knew it.

If she asked and he answered no...

Lord.

In a deep, dark corner of her soul, Lucia Annette Falco almost believed that would be worse.

She inhaled on a shudder, her heart constricting as though it were being squeezed by a giant hand. Acutely aware that her ex-husband was watching her, she tilted her head back and closed her eyes as she'd done earlier.

She felt exhausted. Wan. Weary. As fragile as a blown eggshell, emptied of substance and easy to crush.

Finding her husband locked in an embrace with another woman would have been awful no matter who the woman was, Lucy reflected. But that it had been *Irene Houghton*...

She'd known exactly who Irene was, thanks to Chris's mother. But even had Elizabeth Banks neglected to allude to her son's romantic history with the ex-debutante, Lucy would have recognized the elegantly beautiful blue-eyed blonde.

Irene Houghton had been her nemesis. The embodiment of all the qualities that she, Lucia Annette Falco, had viewed herself as lacking.

Had she been asked ten years ago to define in a single phrase her relationship with Chris, she probably would have said *opposites attract*. The phrase she would have offered had the equation been Chris and Irene was *matched pair*.

Lucy bit her lip, once again trying to shove the past away. This time memory didn't simply resist her efforts. It shoved back.

No, she thought. *Leave me alone.*

She'd wept those words over and over, the night she ran home to her family.

Leave me . . .

She was so tired. The New Year was only a few hours old and she felt as though she'd been slogging through it for a century.

. . . alone.

So tired.

So . . . tired.

Eventually, Lucy slept. And as she slumbered, she dreamed. Not of the worst thing that had ever happened to her, but of one of the most wonderful.

"Lucy . . ." Chris uttered her name in a husky, half-suffocated voice. He managed to trap both her hands with one of his. He used the other to capture her chin and force her to look directly into his eyes. "Sweetheart. Please. *Are you sure?*"

She gazed at him for several seconds, her body thrumming with expectation. Her cheeks felt flushed. Her lips a little swollen. The tips of her breasts ached. So did the delicately petaled flesh between her thighs.

It was two months into their relationship. As delicious as the kissing and cuddling they'd done in the past had been, it was no longer enough. She wanted to belong to Chris in the fullest possible way. And she wanted this to be the night it came to pass.

"Don't you want to?" She infused the question with all the seductiveness at her virginal command. She heard him catch his breath. She watched desire detonate in a shower of topaz and emerald sparks in the depths of his eyes. A thrill of excitement raced through her.

Chris gave a laugh that carried an edge of desperation. Perspiration sheened his brow. "If I wanted to any more, I'd be in pieces!"

"Then let's do it, Chris." She pulled her hands free of his. Lifting her arms, she encircled his neck. Then she snuggled close. "Let's make love."

Again he disengaged and eased her away from him. She was beginning to become more than a little frustrated. But the unsteadiness of his hands—to say nothing of the hard rod of flesh she'd pressed against a few moments ago—kept the emotion in check. The problem obviously was an attack of masculine nobility—something Tina Roberts had once warned could mess up a relationship in a major way, if a girl wasn't extremely careful—rather than a dearth of sexual interest.

"There's only one first time, Lucy," Chris said. "It's not something you can undo afterward."

"I won't want to undo anything afterward," Lucy declared throatily. "I'll only want to do it again." Where these bold words had come from, she wasn't certain. But she had no questions about the source of the next ones. They came straight from her heart. "I love you, Chris. I love you and I want to be with you."

He groaned, his sun-burnished skin pulling tight over his cheekbones. His hold on her altered in the space of a single hammering heartbeat. No longer was he trying to keep her at arm's length. He now seemed to want to fuse their bodies together.

"And I love you," he said, a split second before he took her mouth.

They kissed long and deep. She opened her lips to his tongue, welcoming its rough-velvet invasion. Her skin prickled. Her nipples puckered. A molten heat pooled between her thighs. Somewhere in the back of her mind, she realized that his clever fingers were busy undoing buttons and clasps.

"Chris," she whispered, clutching at the back of his head. "Oh, Chris."

"I need you," he said, lavishing moist, openmouthed kisses up and down her throat. "I need you...so much."

They were on the sofa in the living room of his lakefront apartment. After a few more minutes of increasingly feverish foreplay, Chris muttered something that sounded like "Not here."

Although "here" seemed perfectly fine to Lucy, she didn't protest when he swept her up and carried her into his bedroom. The sensation of being cradled in his arms was too entrancing.

His clothing became a hateful barrier to her. She tried to do something to change the situation. Unfortunately, her hands were shaking so badly that she could scarcely pop the snap on the top of his jeans.

"Oh, God," Chris groaned as her knuckles grazed the denim-covered bulge of his arousal. "Sweetheart. You're killing me. And if I die now...it's going to be as a very unhappy man."

Evading her hands, he stripped himself. The process was fast, but imbued with a certain degree of finesse. Lucy trembled as she drank in the lithe, classically balanced lines of his physique. She also experienced a flash of uniquely feminine trepidation as she saw the potent proof of the need to which he'd admitted only a short time before.

She lifted her eyes to his. His features were taut, like those of an endurance runner in the middle of a marathon. But his expression was the essence of tenderness.

"Second thoughts?" he asked, clearly braced to call a halt if there were.

"Y-yes," she admitted tremulously, realizing it would do her no good to pretend otherwise. "And third and f-fourth and fifth ones."

"Lucy—"

"But it's the first thought that counts," she went on. "I want us to make love, Chris. I want it with all my heart."

He opened his arms. She went to him without hesitation. He lifted her up again and bore her to his bed. After laying her down on the mattress, he began to stroke her. Throat to hip. Hip to throat. She reached up, trying to pull him down into an embrace.

Chris caught her hands and lifted them to his lips. "Wait," he commanded, his warm breath eddying across her knuckles.

But Lucy didn't want to wait. Especially not when it seemed that the waiting meant she had to watch him turn away from her. She levered herself up on her elbows, a protest forming on the tip of her tongue.

The protest dissolved, unspoken, when she saw him pull open the top drawer of a bedside chest and extract a small foil packet.

"You don't h-have to..." she began uncertainly. Earlier in the evening, she'd told him that she'd taken care of her contraceptive needs. Had he not believed her?

"I want to," he said simply. "Two kinds of protection are better than one, sweetheart."

The mattress gave slightly when he finally joined her on the bed. He stretched out beside her and gathered her into his arms. They kissed and caressed. Caressed and kissed.

Lucy licked delicately at a bead of sweat that glistened like a tiny diamond in the hollow at the base of Chris's throat. She breathed in his scent. She nosed his hair-whorled chest, nuzzling against one of his nipples.

He skimmed the line of her collarbone with his lips, then dipped his head to claim the lushly curving flesh below it.

Lucy's breath jammed as her about-to-be lover pleasured her with teeth and tongue. She cried out when she felt his mouth settle over the tip of her right breast and begin to suck.

She was eager. And awkward. And, undeniably, more than a little bit anxious. She tried to speed up the pace. Chris countered by slowing things down. His caresses became slow, searing explorations. His kisses were languid, loving tributes.

"Easy, love," he murmured against her ear. "Don't rush. Don't rush."

"Please . . ."

"Let me feel your hands. Touch me, love."

Compelled by the need in his voice, she did. Tentatively at first, then with increasing confidence. Lucy wanted desperately to please Chris. His responses—the shattered gasps, the sudden shudders—assured her that she did.

The stroke of his fingertips against the entrance to her feminine core made her arch and vibrate like a plucked bowstring. Chis found the nerve-rich nubbin sheltered amid the fragile folds of flesh and teased it very, very gently.

Her hips jerked. She rolled her head back and forth, clutching at the bed linens.

Chris lured her to the edge of fulfillment and held her there for what seemed an eternity before he granted her release. Her body spasmed, racked by a spill of pleasure so intense it was almost beyond endurance.

And then, finally . . .

Lucy felt Chris shift his weight, positioning himself between her legs.

"Open to me, Lucy," he urged in a velvety whisper. "Please. Open to me."

She did.

There was an instant of discomfort as he entered her. A disorienting sense of having lost dominion over her own body. Then came an exquisite feeling of fullness. The solitary ecstasy she'd experienced a few moments before paled in comparison to the consummation this sensation promised.

"Yes." She embraced Chris with her arms and legs, offering everything. This was what she'd wanted. This. With him. Now. "Oh . . . yes."

They moved together, two as one. There was nothing planned about it. Their physical attunement was utterly instinctive. Like yin and yang, they counterbalanced and completed.

"*Lucy—*"

"*Chris—*"

They reached the ultimate peak. Clinging together, they hurtled over.

There were no words.

For a long, long while, there didn't need to be.

"Are you all right?" Chris eventually asked.

"Mmm."

"Is that a yes?"

"Mmm . . . hmm."

He ran a hand down her back, stroking gently against the hollow at the base of her spine. Lucy stirred and pressed a kiss against the side of his neck.

There was a soft, sweet silence. Then Chris said in a meditative tone, "I've never been anyone's first time before."

Lucy laughed a little, not really understanding why. She raised herself up a few inches and gazed down into her lover's face. She smiled teasingly. "Were you nervous?"

"What do you think?" He flushed, suddenly boyish.

She dipped her head and brushed her lips against his. The flavor of his mouth was wickedly familiar. She suspected it might be addictive, too. "If you were," she murmured, "I didn't notice."

He reversed their positions in a sequence of moves Lucy couldn't quite follow.

"If that's the case…" he kissed the tip of her nose "…I was the epitome of calm. Completely in control the whole time."

She laughed again, then surrendered to an impulse she knew was unwise. "Who was *your* first time?"

Chris didn't miss a beat. "At the moment, I can't remember anything that happened before you said the only thing you were going to want to do afterward was do it again."

"All right." Lucy suppressed a sigh. She hadn't really expected him to kiss and tell names. Christopher Dodson Banks was a gentleman. "Forget who. How about when?"

Someone called her name.

"You're asking for a specific date?"

"A general time frame."

Someone called her name a second time. Lucy tried to gesture for quiet, but found she couldn't seem to move her hands.

"End of high school."

Again, her name. It was inflected more imperatively than on the two previous occasions, and followed by an order.

She shifted, trying to figure out why someone who sounded remarkably like the man she was questioning about his romantic history would be telling her to wake up. She *was* up!

Wasn't…she?

"Dammit, Lucy…"

Lucia Annette Falco's wonderful dream smashed head-on into awful reality.

Nine

Finally, Chris thought as his ex-wife jerked awake with a gasp. She looked around, her flushed face revealing a combination of disorientation and dismay.

He'd been angry when Lucy went to sleep on him. He wasn't going to deny that. But he'd understood why she'd sought to shut down, at least temporarily. And angry as he was, he'd intended to let her slumber in peace. He'd even tried to will himself into dropping off.

He'd been right on the verge of dozing, too, when his companion in captivity started to murmur. It had sounded like nonsense at first, so he'd told himself to ignore it. And he had. He'd ignored it right up until the instant she uttered his name in a voice so filled with sensuality that every nerve in his body snapped to attention.

He'd opened his eyes and looked at her. This had been a mistake. A *big* mistake. One glimpse of the unmistakably erotic way Lucy was shifting her hips had kicked his libido into overdrive. The fact that the budding thrust of her nipples was very obvious beneath the wine-colored wool of her dress had done nothing to cool him off.

He'd tried to clamp down on his responses. He'd closed his eyes. He'd clenched his hands. He'd counted aloud, by threes. But the fuse was lit and his imagination fully engaged.

Besides. While he could block sight and sound, he'd had no way to disconnect his nose. The storage room was small. Lucy had been very stimulated. Within a matter of seconds, he'd caught the distinctive scent of her arousal.

He'd endured it as long as he could. But it had soon became throbbingly evident that he was teetering on the brink of a major embarrassment. That was when he'd started calling Lucy's name and ordering her to wake up.

"Wh-what...happened, Chris?" his ex-wife asked throatily. "Why did you wake me up?"

"You were moaning. And moving around."

Her eyes widened. The color in her cheeks intensified. She shifted. Her nostrils flared. The color in her cheeks turned hectic.

The collar of Chris's shirt got very tight. Likewise, the fit of his briefs.

"I was afraid you were having a nightmare," he added, lying through his teeth. He knew perfectly well what she'd been having. And unless he was very much mistaken, she'd just had another one.

Lucy licked her lips, studying him with disconcerting directness. "I'm sorry if I disturbed you."

"You said my name." Chris wondered fleetingly how he would have reacted had it been another man's. He decided he didn't want to know.

"That's why you thought it was a...nightmare?"

"Something like that."

Her mouth curved into a smile that was lush with feminine secrets. Her lashes fluttered down to veil her dark eyes. After a few seconds, she said, "Well, it wasn't."

There was a long silence. A long, *long* silence. Somewhere during the course of it, Chris's pulse rate eased out of potential stroke territory and the fit of his undershorts loosened to the point where he could shift position without worrying about humiliating himself.

Then Lucy squirmed.

"Uh-oh," she muttered, furrowing her brow.

"What?" He was wary.

She lifted her gaze to his, plainly embarrassed. "How do you think Tom, Dick and Butch would respond to a request for a visit to the rest room?"

Chris frowned, suddenly conscious of the pressure of the three cans of soda he'd chugalugged with the pizzas he'd purchased.

"There's only one way to find out," he said. "Let's get them in here and ask."

Lucy glanced at her wristwatch and grimaced. It was 3:46 a.m. on the first day of a brand-new year. She'd been sitting in a toilet stall for nigh on five minutes with no results. It was time to take action.

"Tom?"

"Yeah?"

"Would you turn on the tap, please?"

"Oh, uh, sure. Hot or cold?"

"Your choice."

"Oh. Okay. I'm, uh, gonna do hot. Here goes."

Yes, she thought gratefully as the gush of running water started to work its magic.

"I'm really sorry I have to stand in here, Lucy." The tone was plaintive. "But Butch said, since there's a window..."

"It's okay, Tom," she responded, wondering how many more times he was going to apologize.

"I'm keepin' my fingers in my ears, so I don't really hear anything."

"That's very considerate of you."

"Huh?"

"That's very. . ." She broke off, stifling a sudden yawn.

"Lucy?"

"Nothing, Tom. Nothing. Tell me a little more about you and Dick and Dora-Jean."

"I told you mostly everything. Dora-Jean divorced Dick 'cause he paid her too much attention and she divorced me 'cause I guess I ignored her. Then she married and divorced Dick again because I don't exactly know why except maybe she didn't have anything better to do. This isn't bad-mouthin' her, but sometimes it's really hard to figure out what Dora-Jean wants, you know? I'm not even sure *she's* sure."

Lucy experienced a twinge of emotional kinship. "That happens."

"Can I tell you the rest of our escape plan now? 'Cause it really is a planned plan."

"Sure, Tom."

"How far did I get before?"

"Uh…" Lucy tried to recall. The bearded Mr. Spivey had started chattering about the plan out of nervousness, she suspected. Still feeling the aftershocks from her incredibly erotic dream—as well as trying to cope with the emotions roiled up by some of the things Chris and she had said to each other—she hadn't really listened.

"Oh, I know!" Tom announced excitedly. "I was tellin' you about how we made a list of the countries where you can go and they won't send you back."

"Right."

Her mind started to drift after the first three or four words. Her thoughts weren't terribly coherent, but they all revolved around her ex-husband. She also kept returning to the realization that she and Chris probably had talked more intensely—more *openly*—during the past eleven or so hours than they had during their entire marriage. She'd vented feelings she'd scarcely been aware of having. She'd told truths she'd taken more than a decade to discover.

She suspected— No. She *knew*. She knew that Chris had done the same.

But for all the openness and intensity, they hadn't spoken of what had happened ten days before their first wedding anniversary. Not . . . yet.

Lucy drew a shaky breath, knitting her fingers together, then pulling them apart. The question was hers to ask. Or not to ask. It was plain that Chris had left the final decision up to her. It wasn't emotional cowardice on his part, of that she was sure. Instead, it seemed to be a form of—

"I don't *believe* this!" It was Dick Spivey. He was inside the rest room, and he sounded furious. "You told Lucy our *entire* escape plan?"

Uh-oh, she thought with a guilty grimace.

"So what if I did?" Tom's tone wavered between defiance and anxiety.

"So what? So what? So you've wrecked *everything,* you dimwit!"

"Oh, yeah?"

"Yeah! Do you know how mad Butch is going to be?"

"B-B-Butch?" The defiance was gone. Anxiety gave way to something more acute.

"Uh-huh, Butch. We worked *weeks* planning this escape route! We cashed in all our frequent-flier miles. I even used those coupons me and Dora-Jean were saving for our, uh, second second honeymoon! And now it's all *ruined!* We're going to have to cancel everything, Tom! Do you hear me? Every single solitary thing! We're probably going to have to *hitchhike* out of the country! Or take a *bus*—"

"No! No! You promised we were gonna fly in first class! With free champagne!"

"Forget first class." The tone was trenchant. "And forget the fancy restaurants and big suites. It's gonna be greasy spoons and roach motels for us, because you couldn't keep your mouth shut!"

"But *why?*"

"Because Lucy will tell the police everything!"

Lucy froze in the act of peeling off her ruined panty hose. It had never even occurred to her, she thought, pressing her lips together to hold back a semihysterical giggle. She'd let ninety-nine and nine-tenths percent of Tom's babbling go in one ear and out the other.

Chris would have been taking notes, she told herself. And he would have been asking cogent questions. He would have found out all there was to know about the escape plan and then some.

She shook her head despairingly. She'd gone beyond the soft-touch stage and into mush-brain territory.

"So?"

"So, blabbermouth, if we do any of our escape plan, they'll be able to catch us! They'll be waiting for us!"

There was a long pause.

"Lucy wouldn't do that," Tom finally asserted. Then he raised his voice and demanded, *"Lucy!* Tell Dick you wouldn't do that!"

She gulped. "Uh—"

"The police would make her do it," Dick declared fiercely.

"They would?"

Lucy bit her lower lip, thinking hard. A fragment of the conversation she'd had with Wayne Dweck skittered through her brain. Then a tidbit of the one she'd had with Jimmy Burns. Oddly enough, it triggered the memory of Butch Johnson's explanation of how he'd ended up doing time for burglary.

She stiffened suddenly. Her heart skipped a beat. Maybe two.

What if—?

No, she quickly told herself. It would never work. Only an idiot would fall for such a transparent—

Oh.

Oh...my.

Hmm.

Well, maybe it could work after all.

"There's only one way to find out," she whispered.

"Lucy?" It was Dick.

"Just a sec," she called back, tidying her clothes and fluffing her hair.

"We sort of have a problem." It was Tom. A very glum-sounding Tom.

Lucy took a slow, steadying breath, then squared her shoulders and unlocked the bathroom stall. Flinging open the door with a flourish, she stepped out. The tiled floor was cool against the soles of her feet.

"Tom and Dick," she began, consciously mimicking the confidently coaxing inflections of Tiffany Tarrington Toulouse, "I understand you have some trouble with your travel plans."

The Spivey brothers looked at her.

They looked at each other.

Then they looked back at her.

Finally, they nodded.

"Well, guys..." Lucia Annette Falco spread her hands in a *ta-da!* gesture. "*I'm* a travel professional!"

Although he generally tried to steer clear of gender stereotyping, Chris *did* subscribe to the notion that women took longer rest room breaks than men. Thus, he was not particularly surprised that he was able to go to the john and back and be tied up again by Butch before Lucy returned from her visit to the loo.

The fact that she was still absent after ten minutes triggered some concern.

What if she's gotten ill? he asked himself, remembering her earlier pallor. Or had an accident? Damp rest room tiles could be treacherous, especially in stockinged feet. She'd seemed a wee bit wobbly when Tom had escorted her out.

Concern metastasized into fear at the end of twenty minutes. It was obvious that something was wrong.

What if he'd driven her into making some sort of escape bid? Chris demanded of himself. Why hadn't he shown her some sensitivity? Why hadn't he cut her some slack? They were being held prisoner, for God's sake! Granted, their captors seemed more dangerous to themselves than to anybody else. But still! He should have offered his ex-wife upbeat and encouraging conversation, not handed her can after newly opened can of emotional worms!

His mood spiraled downward. What if Tom and Dick and Butch weren't as harmless as they appeared? Lucy was an intensely alluring woman. What if one of them—

He'd kill him, Chris thought savagely. If any of those bastards dared to touch Lucy, he'd rip the guy's heart out.

At twenty-one minutes after his ex-wife's departure from the storage room, Christopher Dodson Banks started yelling for help.

He was still yelling fifteen minutes later, when Tom Spivey opened the storage room door and gestured Lucy inside.

"What's *wrong* with you, Chris?" The question was cranky. "Jeez, Louise! Do you have any idea how tough it is to make an entire new escape plan when you've got some guy hollerin' for help in the next room? Poor Lucy could hardly concentrate at her computer!"

Chris barely registered a word of this ridiculous recitation. He was focused on his ex-wife. To say that she had returned to him safe and sound didn't begin to tell the story. She looked . . . incandescent.

Her cheeks were flushed with excitement. Her dark eyes were dancing. The curve of her rosy mouth made him think of cats and cream and canary feathers.

For one dizzying split second, it also made him think of kisses. Then he stomped out the reaction and kicked it away.

"I was . . . concerned," he finally managed to explain, looking up at Tom.

"About what?"

"Lucy was gone a long time."

Tom regarded him blankly. "Well, yeah," he finally conceded, scratching his chin. "I suppose. But you knew she was with us, right?"

Chris glanced at Lucy. Her expression told him to let it go. He did.

"Right," he agreed, transferring his gaze back to the bearded Spivey brother. "I guess I'm starting to get a little stressed out."

"Oh, you gotta watch that. Stress can kill you. Try takin' deep breaths." Tom demonstrated, hyperventilating to the point of wooziness.

"*Tom!*" Lucy exclaimed, preventing him toppling over.

"Whuh . . . whuh h-happened?"

"You need to go outside and sit down, Tom," Lucy said firmly. "You've been working very, very hard. You should take a break."

The bearded man blinked several times, then shook his head. "I . . . I gotta tie you up first, Lucy."

"No." She patted his arm, maneuvering him toward the door. "You don't have to tie me up."

"Yes, I do. It's like a . . . uh . . . rule."

"But I'm your accomplice now, remember?"

Chris nearly choked.

"Yeah," Tom conceded, his brow furrowing. "I remember."

"You don't tie up your accomplices, Tom. That's a rule, too. Trust me."

"Oh . . . 'kay."

"Thank you. Now go take a break. Have another slice of pizza."

A moment later, Tom Spivey was out the door. A moment after that, Lucy was kneeling beside Chris, undoing his bonds.

"Are you sure you should be doing this?" he asked. Her proximity—to say nothing of the brush of her fingers—was playing merry hell with his pulse. "I'm not one of their accomplices."

She flashed him a feisty smile. His breathing pattern snarled. "You can be mine, okay?"

"Uh..." He swallowed. "Sure."

"Were you really worried about me?"

"Is this a trick question?"

Although she flashed another smile, he saw a hint of warning in her eyes. "I can take care of myself, Chris."

"I know that," he said after a few seconds. "But that doesn't mean I don't feel the need to worry. Or... the instinct to protect you."

Lucy went still. Her gaze slid away from his. "Is that why you tried to make Butch let me go?"

His right hand was free. He lifted it and touched her cheek. He felt a small tremor of reaction go through her at the contact.

"Do you want me to apologize if it was?" He forced himself to lower his hand.

She moistened her lips. "No," she said throatily. "I don't."

Chris began undoing the restraints on his left hand. "Was that the other reason you insisted on staying with me?" he asked carefully. "Besides your feeling this is all your fault, I mean? Did you want me to understand you can take care of yourself?"

He raised his eyes to hers as he spoke. She sustained his gaze steadily for several moments, then said, "Something like that. Yes."

His left hand came free. He rubbed one wrist, then the other. The impulse to pursue this subject was strong. But so was the memory of how he'd berated himself during Lucy's absence.

Upbeat and encouraging conversation, he ordered. *No more cans of worms until this is over. Long over.*

"Would you like to tell me about the new escape plan?" he inquired dryly.

Her entire demeanor changed. Her face lit up with mirth. Her eyes fizzed. For a crazy instant, he found himself flashing back on their wedding night. She'd worn the same intoxicating—and intoxicated?—expression then.

Oh, Lucy, he thought. *Maybe you were as drunk on our love as I was.*

"Well," she began, hooking a lock of hair behind her left ear. "Their original escape plan had to be trashed, because Tom told me all about it while I was sitting in a stall in the ladies' room."

"He was in the ladies' room with you." Chris kept his tone neutral.

Lucy gestured his concern aside. "He was more embarrassed than I was. Butch insisted he go in and guard me, because there's a window in there. I was actually kind of flattered."

"Flattered?"

"That Butch would think I could get my size-twelve hips through what's barely a size-six opening."

"Ah."

"Anyway. Dick charged in as Tom was finishing up spilling the escape plan and threw a hissy fit. The theme of it being that everything was ruined because I'd tell the police and they'd be captured."

Chris decided to let the issue of Dick's entrance into the ladies' room pass. He cocked his head and asked, "Would you?"

"What? Tell the police their escape plans?"

"Mmm."

Lucy smiled ruefully. "I didn't really listen to much of what Tom had to say."

He had to laugh. "I can't imagine why."

"I think I'm afraid he's going to start making sense to me, you know?"

"God forbid!"

"In any case, the Spivey brothers started fighting."

"Again."

"Exactly. But this was really bad. I had the feeling things might get seriously out of hand. So I tried to figure out a way of defusing things."

Chris narrowed his eyes, contemplating the truly lunatic scenario that had just popped into his head. "Don't tell me," he said slowly. "You came out of the bathroom stall, reminded Tom and Dick they just happened to be in the presence of the office manager of Gulliver's Travels and offered to book them the escape plan of a lifetime."

Lucy dimpled. "More or less, yes."

"Seriously?"

"What do you think?"

The temptation to tease was overwhelming. "Well, we *have* established that you're an incredibly soft touch."

"Chris!"

"And there *is* the possibility of Stockholm syndrome."

"Stockholm syn—? You mean where hostages start identifying with their captors? Oh, please!"

"You did say Tom Spivey was starting to make sense to you."

"I said I was *afraid* he was going to start making sense to me!" Lucy frowned at him. He fought to keep his face straight. He failed. She took a swat at him. "Oh, you!"

He held up his hands in mock surrender, relishing having the freedom to move them again. "Okay, okay. So you didn't really book the, uh, getaway of a lifetime for our favorite trio of criminals. What, exactly, did you do?"

"*Pretended* to book the you-know-what for you-know-who. I even printed out itineraries and tickets. But I transposed all the reservations codes, so nothing actually got entered in the system."

"In other words, you set them up."

"You could use those words, I suppose."

"You probably—what? Conned them into thinking they'll be flying the Concorde and staying at the Connaught?"

"Private Learjet and the Caesar's Palace in Vegas."

"Now, *I'm* starting to feel sorry for them!"

She smiled provocatively. "There's more."

"I shudder to think."

"You remember the computer whiz kid I talked about when we were at the hotel bar?"

It took him a second to dredge up the name. "Wayne Dweck. The one with the crush on, uh . . . Tiffington Tally-something."

"Tiffany Tarrington Toulouse." A look of wonderment shimmered through Lucy's lovely eyes. "You . . . you really listened to me, didn't you?"

The urge to touch assailed him. He battled it down. "I hope I'm learning to."

Her mouth trembled. For a second or so, he thought she might utter the question he knew had to be asked and answered if there was to be any chance of their reconciling. But she backed off, lowering her gaze.

"Tell me the 'more,' Lucy," he prompted gently, accepting her decision.

She inhaled deeply, her breasts rising with the breath. She expelled the air in a steady stream, then looked at him once again.

"Well," she began, clearly striving to recapture the bantering tone she'd been using, "Wayne's installed an E-mail encryption system at his workstation. I just happened to pick that workstation when I sat down to program the great escape. And in between making pretend plane and hotel reservations, I messaged everyone on Wayne's E-mail list for help."

"In code." She was incredible, he thought. Absolutely . . . incredible.

"It was the only way I could think of. I had to type in the message with Tom and Dick peering over my shoulder. The way Wayne has his system set up, the sender can post the entry on his or her screen in plaintext or scrambled, depending on which function key is struck."

"And you struck scrambled."

"Uh-huh."

"And then you sent your 'help' message to—what?—hundreds of people?"

"Thousands, maybe. Millions, even. Wayne's deeply committed to being a citizen of cyberspace."

"What was the message?"

"'Help. Being held hostage in Gulliver's Travels, Atlanta.'"

Emotion started to build within Chris. He struggled to keep it in check. "Short and to the point."

"I thought I'd better keep it simple." Lucy grimaced. "The only problem is, the person on the other end has to have the key to break the code."

"Do you think Wayne's on his own E-mail list?" He couldn't take his eyes off his ex-wife. He was mesmerized by her.

"That's what I'm hoping."

Chris's mind reached back and snagged something Lucy had said a minute ago. "You did this with Tom and Dick breathing down your neck?"

She shrugged off any suggestion of risk. "I could have typed in a plaintext petition to the director of the FBI, for all they would have noticed."

"And what about Butch?"

"Remember his story about how he got captured during a burglary?"

"Vividly."

"Well . . ." The fizz returned to her eyes, the feisty smile to her lips. ". . . one of our other travel agents happens to have this fiendishly complicated game with death beams, invading aliens and the scum of the universe installed on his computer."

"Which you just happened to boot up when Butch was looking."

She nodded demurely. "What do you think?"

What did he think?

The emotion within Chris reached critical mass. All his pledges of self-restraint went by the boards. He lifted his hands and caged Lucy's face, sliding his fingers back through her hair.

"I think you're the most amazing woman it's ever been my privilege to know," he said huskily. "I still love you, sweetheart. I never stopped."

And then he kissed her.

Ten

It was auld lang syne and a whole lot more.

Sense memory overwhelmed Lucy. Appetites whetted by her dream clamored avidly for satiation. Desire sang through her blood and sizzled along the synapses of her brain. She shivered in voluptuous response to the man with whom she'd once resolved to live happily ever after.

The taste of his lips...

The feel of his hands...

The primal scent of his flesh...

She didn't submit to the kiss. She didn't succumb or surrender to it, either. For a few mad moments, she enlisted in it as an equal, giving as ardently as she received.

And then sanity—emotional sobriety—returned.

"No!" she cried, breaking free of her ex-husband's embrace and pushing him away. "Leave me alone!"

The throbbing emptiness between her thighs and the terrible ache in her heart made a mockery of her words, but

Lucy told herself they didn't matter. She staggered to her feet, rubbing her mouth with the back of her hand.

"Lucy." Chris got to his feet, as well, his face pale and intent. He reached out for her.

"Don't touch me!" She warded him off with a gesture.

"Sweetheart, please—"

"And don't call me that!" She was shaking like the victim of a raging fever. Her eyes stung. She was desperately afraid that she was going to start to weep. "How could you? How could you do that?"

"I had to, Lucy. I couldn't stop myself."

"You should have!"

"I should have done a lot of things." His tone was stark.

She glared at him, still fighting off tears.

Ask him, something deep within her suddenly urged. *You'll be a prisoner of what happened for the rest of your life if you don't.*

"Ask me, Lucy," he said, seeming to read her mind. "Please. After all these years. After all the pain. Ask me."

She knew she had to.

"Did you sleep with Irene Houghton after we were married?"

She saw his hazel eyes flicker at her phrasing. Then she saw him shake his head. A lock of sandy-brown hair fell forward onto his brow. He shoved it back into place with a brusque movement.

"No," he answered, sustaining her gaze levelly. "I didn't. I swear to you, Lucy. If I've earned back even a shred of your trust during the time we've been locked up in here...please. Believe me. *I didn't.*"

"I saw you kissing her." She saw it again in her mind's eye as she spoke. Christopher Dodson Banks and Irene Houghton. Her husband and the woman who had seemed to personify everything she wasn't.

His face tightened, the angles of his handsome features growing more acute, the lines that bracketed his flexible mouth deepening. "I know you did," he told her quietly. "You were supposed to."

Lucy took an involuntary step backward, raising a shaking hand to trembling lips. This was a cruelty she hadn't anticipated. Was he actually saying that he'd done it on *purpose?*

"I was...s-supposed...to?" She could barely get the words out.

"The receptionist at the firm buzzed me when you arrived. I knew you were heading toward my office. I wanted you to see."

"Why?"

Chris took a deep breath, like a parachutist preparing for an odds-defying plunge. Then he said, with almost no inflection, "It was the only way I could think of to get your attention."

A wild laugh bubbled up Lucy's throat. She choked it back, knowing that hysteria would not be far behind if she let it out.

"Why not put up a billboard?" she demanded scathingly. "Or scream at me? Or...or..." Anguish gripped her. *"...stab me in the heart?"*

She saw shame in his compelling eyes. And pain that seemed to match her own. What she didn't see was an inclination to retreat from the truth. She'd asked, and Chris was obviously intent on answering in full.

She didn't know if she could bear it.

"I was jealous, Lucy."

It took her a moment to process this unadorned assertion. Her mind seemed determined to reject it.

"Jealous?" she finally repeated. She shook her head. It made no sense! She'd been faithful to Chris in thought, word and deed. How could he possibly have suspected otherwise? "Of what, Chris? Of *who?"*

"Just about everybody in your life."

"Wh-what?"

"When we came back from our honeymoon, it seemed like you and me against the world. Less than six months later, making time for me—for *us*—was barely on your to-do list."

"That's not fair!"

But even as she made the protest, Lucy was assailed by a wave of guilt. She'd reordered her entire pattern of existence following her marriage, without even thinking about the implications of what she was doing. She'd let her marital identity supersede her single one in every way that counted. Being Mrs. Christopher Dodson Banks—pleasing her husband, fitting into his world—had been all she cared about. The dreams she'd had of doing by herself, to herself, for herself, had been transmuted.

Then, late one April afternoon, she'd found herself mooning around their apartment like a lovesick adolescent girl as the watch on her wrist tick-tick-ticked its way past the hour at which Chris had vaguely promised he'd call her from work, and she'd felt a jolt of panic. *What's going on here?* she'd asked herself, shaken by her behavior. *I haven't done this praying-for-the-phone-to-ring ritual since... since... since...*

Well, in point of fact, she'd never done it! And she'd always felt vaguely sorry for the members of her gender who did.

Chris had rung shortly thereafter with a terse message that they'd have to forgo the evening out they'd discussed, because he had to work late. She'd tried to engage him in a conversation, but he'd begged off.

The following day, she'd lunched with Elizabeth Banks at an uncomfortably la-di-da restaurant. Chris's mother had started quizzing her about where she got her hair done, where she bought her clothes and why she seemed so disinterested in an upcoming gala for a charity with which the Banks family had long been associated. Lucy had left the tête-à-tête feeling unattractive, inadequate, and more than

a little angry. Not so much with the older woman as with
herself.

What's going on here? she'd demanded once again.

Acting on impulse, she'd headed back to her home
neighborhood and stopped in at Falco's Pizzeria. Her
brothers and father had treated her as though they hadn't
seen her for ten years. So, too, had a number of the restaurant's regular customers. In the midst of their fussing, Tina
Roberts had dropped by and made some not-so-veiled al-
lusions about what happened to girls who married up and
out and forgot who they really, truly were.

She'd tried to talk about what had happened to Chris that
night. He'd looked at her as though she were speaking to
him in Swahili. She'd pressed the issue. He'd distracted her
with kisses. And caresses. And before she realized what was
happening, they'd been sprawled on the living room sofa...

He'd taken her to ecstasy and back. But in the quivering
aftermath of physical fulfillment, she'd felt as though she'd
been on the receiving end of a "Yeah, yeah, I hear what
you're tellin' me, babe" brush-off. Old insecurities—and
more than a few nasty new ones—had raised their ugly
heads.

She'd picked a fight with Chris the next morning about
absolutely nothing. Or, rather, she'd tried to. Her cool and
self-possessed husband hadn't risen to a single piece of bait.
It had been infuriating.

Lucia Annette Falco had reasserted herself shortly thereafter.

"Fair or not," Chris said flatly, responding to her previous words, "it's what I felt. You were there for Vinnie after
he broke his collarbone. You were there for Mikey and Joey
when they needed their egos pumped up. You were there for
your uncle Aldo after his wife ran off with that dance in-
structor. You were there for those girls you started tutoring
in math on Thursday nights at the Y, and for the old folks
at that nursing home you visited on alternate—"

"They *needed* me, Chris!" she burst out.

"And I didn't?"

His tone hit her like a karate chop to the windpipe, temporarily depriving her of the ability to breathe. Lucy gulped once. Twice.

Ten years ago, she would have said no, he hadn't. She would have said the same ten minutes—ten *seconds!*—ago, as well. But now...

She'd always perceived Chris as being strong and sure and self-sufficient. He wasn't overtly arrogant, yet confidence seemed the hallmark of everything he did, And it was an inner confidence. It didn't rely on external validation. He knew who and what he was.

She'd been drawn to him because of this. There was no denying that. But she'd begun to resent his certainty after a time, because it contrasted so sharply with the confusion roiling within her.

"I...I don't know," she finally admitted. "Did you?"

"I needed you more than I've ever needed anyone. You filled up places I didn't know were empty."

Her heart seemed to stop. "You never said—"

"I couldn't, dammit! I come from a family where people don't admit to needing, Lucy. A Banks isn't supposed to let down, break down or stick out his hand for assistance, because a Banks isn't supposed to have any weaknesses. I didn't have the words. And even if I had, I probably couldn't have brought myself to utter them." Chris paused, his lips twisting as though he were in pain. "Except in bed. I could talk about needing when we were together in bed."

"Because it was...sex?"

Temper flashed in his eyes. Swift. Sudden. Like a streak of summer lightning. She quailed slightly at the sight of it, but stood her ground. "It was more than that, and you know it."

There was a long silence. The emotions that had spiked between them seemed to flatten, just a little bit.

"You thought there was a problem with our marriage?" Lucy finally asked.

He nodded.

"You knew *I* thought there was a problem."

He nodded again.

"Then why... why did you say no when I brought up the possibility of our getting some counseling? Another Banks family taboo?"

"That was part of it. But the main reason I rejected the idea was that I didn't think the problem was me. And even if it was—" he smiled bitterly "—I had the twisted notion that you were supposed to fix it."

Lucy shifted her weight. Chris was speaking solely in the past tense, she realized, conscious of a slight acceleration in the pace of her heartbeat. Did that mean—?

"What... what do you think now?" she questioned carefully.

"Are you asking whether I've changed my mind?"

It was her turn to nod.

Her ex-husband gazed at her wordlessly for several seconds, then quietly replied, "Yes. It's taken me a hell of a long time to do it. But yes. I've changed my mind."

"I... see."

"Do you, Lucy?"

She blinked at the challenging tone of the query, her throat tightening. "I—I want to," she finally managed. "I want to understand what went wrong between us and why. Otherwise..."

She couldn't finish. She couldn't contemplate the alternative.

Chris expelled a breath and forked a hand through his hair. "Look," he began. "I'm not going to try to justify that scene with Irene. Or make excuses for it. What I did was wrong. It was...*stupid*. But my intention wasn't to drive you away, Lucy. God! That's the last thing I wanted. What I wanted to do was to get you back. To get *us* back."

"And to do that, you had to get me to pay attention."

"Yes."

"So you got Irene Houghton to stage a scene with you." She frowned inwardly as she spoke, dimly aware that there was something...off...about this assertion. Her visit to Chris's office ten days before their anniversary had been an impulsive one. They'd had a spat the previous evening about the amount of time she'd been spending trying to mediate a business disagreement between her father and her brother Vinnie. She'd wanted to smooth things over. How could Chris have solicited help in staging a scene he didn't even know would occur?

Her ex-husband's gray-green eyes widened with something close to shock.

"No!" he denied, making a slashing gesture with one hand. "Irene had no clue what I was doing. She'd come into the firm to see one of the senior partners about some business matter, and she stopped by my office to say hello. She'd been there about ninety seconds when the receptionist buzzed to say you'd arrived. That's when the idea came to me."

"The idea of kissing her and letting me see."

"It was an impulse, Lucy. The most misguided impulse I've ever had. But I acted on it."

Lucy let a few seconds go by, trying to digest everything he'd told her. It wasn't easy. Then she asked, "What did you think I was going to do, Chris? How did you think I was going to react when I walked in and found you wrapped around another woman?"

And not just any other woman. Oh, no. Irene Houghton!

"I don't know that I really 'thought' anything." The response was laced with self-disgust. "If I did, I definitely didn't think it through. I basically expected you to take it as a challenge. To stand up and fight."

"For y-you." The pronoun snagged briefly in her throat as she considered the implications of what he'd just said.

"For us." He grimaced. "*My* version of us, at least."

"But instead of standing up and fighting, I ran away."

"While I watched like a fool, wondering what had gone wrong." Chris shook his head, his eyes bleak. "I pretty much lost it when I found out you'd gone back to your family. I told myself I'd been right. That when push came to shove, you'd chosen them over me. The deal was sealed when I tried to come and talk to you and your brothers and father told me you'd told them there was nothing to be said."

"Oh, Chris..." Her rejection of Chris's overture had been a matter of anger and hurt. It had also been a test. Had her then-husband been willing to fight his way through the Falco male gauntlet to get to her, she would have taken it as a sign that he still cared. But he hadn't, and she'd been forced to conclude that he'd chosen Irene—or at least what Irene symbolized—over her.

"If I could go back and undo what I did, I would," Chris said painfully. "But I can't. I can only tell you what I've told you about a dozen times already. I'm sorry, Lucy. I'm so, so sorry."

She blinked against a renewed threat of tears. "I'm sorry, too."

"No." He was adamant. "*No!* You have nothing to be sorry for."

"Yes, I do!" Chris had been right when he said what he'd done couldn't be excused. But it could be put into context and understood. And doing so required that she face up to her own misguided impulses and mistakes in judgment. "I got so caught up in reacting to how our marriage was affecting me that I stopped asking myself how it might be affecting you. And you made that easy, Chris. Because the more time passed, the less you seemed to feel about anything. I was so sure about us when I made that New Year's Eve resolution about our living happily ever after. Only afterward... God! I got so confused about what that meant and how I—*we*—were supposed to do it. There were moments when you and I were like one person. When I couldn't separate us—*me*—out. And that was scary. There were other moments when there didn't seem to be any connection at all. That was pretty frightening, too."

She sucked in a breath, wondering if she was making any sense at all. The words were pouring out, geysering up from deep within her.

"I should have stood up for us and our marriage—for *myself*—that night in your office," she said fiercely. "I think I would have, if you'd been with anyone but Irene Houghton. Because when I saw you with h-h-her..." Lucy broke off abruptly, her control starting to crack. "When I saw that, *I* pretty much lost it. All I could think was that Irene was everything I wasn't. That she was exactly the kind of w-woman you were *supposed* to fall in love with and marry. I d-didn't take it as a challenge, Chris. I took it as a competition. A competition I... had ... n-no chance... of w-w-winning."

Lucy started to cry. The tears she'd tried so hard to hold back welled up and spilled over her lower eyelids. They were tears of regret and remorse, mostly. But they carried a tincture of relief, too.

As Chris had said, they couldn't go back and undo what had been done. But at long, long last, they'd spoken the truth about it.

"Oh, L-Lucy." Her ex-husband gathered her into his arms, hugging her close and stroking her back. His voice was thick. His hands were trembling. "Oh, sweetheart. Please. Don't."

"I tried to h-hate you," she admitted on a broken sob. "And then I tried to be...b-be indifferent. But I c-couldn't. I *can't*. I love y-you. Still. Always." She eased back slightly, lifting her gaze to meet Chris's once again. His gray-green eyes seemed preternaturally bright. "Only it's not the s-same as before, Chris. Because *I'm* not the same."

She watched her ex-husband's well-shaped mouth curve into a smile of infinite tenderness. Impervious though he once might have appeared to her, he definitely did not look that way now.

"I'm not the same as I was, either," he told her huskily, gently brushing the tears from her cheeks. "At least, I hope I'm not. Because the man I used to be didn't understand what kind of love is required for two people to live happily ever after. But the man I am now—"

The slow, seamless swoon begun by Lucia Annette Falco's heart in response to Christopher Dodson Banks's words rebounded into a startled flip-flop at the sound of the storage room door swinging open.

The intruder was Dick Spivey.

The first sentence out of his mouth was a complaint about Butch Johnson's refusal to stop battling aliens from a parallel universe and go back to stealing the Red Treasure.

The second was an angry demand to know what the hell Chris had "shared" to make her cry.

"Thank you," Chris said about fifteen minutes later, when it was once again just him and Lucy in the storage room.

"For what?"

"For saving me from grievous bodily harm at the hands of Tom, Dick and Percival."

His ex-wife laughed and snuggled up against him. "They weren't serious about that."

"You think not?" He teased a lock of his companion's hair, savoring the yielding warmth of her body. The demons of the past had finally been dragged out and exorcised, he told himself. The future beckoned. "They looked pretty serious to me."

"I'm positive. Once they realized I was crying because I was happy, not because you'd 'shared' something horrible, they were thrilled. They were just trying to make certain your intentions fit their definition of *honorable*."

"And a surprisingly inelastic definition it is, all things considered."

"Well..." Lucy felt herself flush.

"Do you think they were persuaded? About the honorable nature of my intentions, I mean."

"Pretty much."

"Are you?" He shifted to get a clearer look at her face. He'd spoken of remarriage. He hadn't really gotten a response.

Lucy regarded him solemnly for several seconds. Then she gave him a smile that arrowed straight to his heart. "Absolutely."

They kissed.

Softly. Sweetly.

They kissed again.

Harder this time, and with considerably more heat.

"Mmm..." Lucy breathed.

"I'll second that," he concurred, nipping at her lower lip. It would be different between them this time, he vowed. Different...meaning better.

They said nothing for more than a minute. The silence was fluidly companionable, not cast in concrete. It resonated with a spirit of reunion.

"Why didn't we do this before?" Lucy eventually asked.

"What?" Chris countered. "Get ourselves taken hostage and stashed in a storage room by a trio of numbskulls?"

"No." She laughed and made a droll face. Then her expression turned serious, her eyes gazing deeply into his. "Why didn't we *talk*, Chris?"

"We talked," he contradicted. "Sometimes. At least we tried to. But we kept most of the things that should have been said to ourselves. We also didn't...listen...very well."

"You listened better than I did."

"*Lucy—*"

She stopped his lips with her fingers. "No. Really," she insisted. "This isn't me trying to take on the burdens of the world or shoulder all the blame. Back at the very beginning, when we were first going out, you paid attention to me when we had conversations. It was very...sexy."

He lifted an eyebrow. His body stirred. "Oh, really?"

"Mmm-hmm. Although there *were* times I worried you might be feigning an admiration for my brain in order to get to my, ah—" she moved her hand in a provocative gesture "—whatever."

"You're not worried about that anymore, are you?"

She dimpled.

"Good," he said firmly. "Because you actually had it backward. I was feigning interest in your 'whatever' to get to your brain!"

They both laughed. Then they kissed a third time. The melding of their mouths was playful at first, but quickly tilted into passion. Neither one of them was breathing steadily when the embrace finally came to an end.

"I just wish we hadn't waited ten years," Lucy said huskily, toying with one of the buttons on his shirt. Once impeccably white and perfectly pressed, the garment was now more than a little worse for wear. "We've wasted so much time—"

Chris trapped her hand and pressed it flat against his chest. "No waste, Lucy. We made use of those ten years. We used them to change. To grow. We're finally ready for each other."

Eleven

Although nearly everything of importance had been said, Lucy and Chris went on talking for another thirty minutes or so. Eventually, however, the strain of their shared ordeal began to tell. The pauses between sentences lengthened. Yawns became more frequent. Eyelids drooped lower. And lower. And lower still. Finally, they closed completely, and stayed that way.

"Love...you," Lucia Annette Falco murmured as awareness slipped away and slumber enveloped her.

"Love you...too," Christopher Dodson Banks tenderly replied, cuddling her close to his heart.

They slept. He, leaning against one of the storage room walls. She, nestled against his chest.

What they dreamed of while they slept was not auld lang syne. As befitted the first day of a brand-new year, what they dreamed of was their future.

* * *

Lucy awoke with a crick in her back and a sublimely happy feeling of anticipation in her heart. She stirred languorously within the protective circle of her ex-husband's arms, wincing a bit at the knot in her spine. Tilting her head up, she slowly opened her eyes.

She found Chris looking down at her. While the expression she saw on his face didn't immediately uncramp her muscles, the rush of heat it sent coursing through her body served as a very effective analgesic.

"Good morning," he said softly, brushing a lock of hair back from her forehead.

It took her a few moments to scrape together enough breath to respond to this greeting. "Good m-morning," she finally returned.

Chris's gaze held hers for several heady seconds, then drifted downward to her mouth. Lucy felt a flutter of response deep within her. Her lips parted on an involuntary sigh.

"I want to kiss you," he admitted with a hint of ruefulness, his eyes returning to hers. "But I'm afraid my oral hygiene leaves something to be desired. My teeth and tongue seem a bit . . . mossy."

Lucy understood perfectly. She, too, was experiencing the consequences of having gone nearly twenty-fours hours without brushing, flossing or gargling. She vaguely remembered having popped a breath mint after lunch the day before, but its freshening effects had long since worn off.

Still . . .

"I don't mind if you don't," she stated frankly, then gave a throaty laugh. "Because I'd very much like to be kissed."

Chris's eyes sparked emerald green, but he didn't immediately move to take advantage of her willingness. Tracing the curve of her right cheek with the tip of the index finger of his left hand, he asked, "Are you sure?"

"Positive." Lucy stroked up the front of his shirt, relishing the ripple and release of the firmly muscled flesh beneath the rumpled white fabric. "It's like lovers and eating garlic. As long as *both* parties do it, there's no problem."

"Oh, really?"

"Oh, yes." She slid her hands over his shoulders and around his neck "Really. It's one of those things anyone who's ever worked in an Italian restaurant knows."

They kissed. Tentatively at first, then with increasing conviction. Lucy shivered as Chris nipped at her lower lip with the edge of his teeth. A moment later, she felt the sinuous lick of his tongue and whimpered softly.

She opened to him, her fingers spasming against his nape. This time, he was swift to accept what she was offering.

The kiss deepened.

"Lucy..."

"Chris..."

He caressed down her back, his hands coming to rest at the base of her spine. He coaxed her closer. She arched into the embrace, headily aware of the hard rise of his masculinity against her upper leg.

Yes, Lucy thought, angling her head to allow Chris even more intimate access. *Oh...yes...*

The threat of hypoxia finally forced them to ease apart a couple of inches. A shared awareness that they were very vulnerable to interruption kept them from renewing the kiss and allowing it to escalate to its natural conclusion.

"I don't suppose there's any way we could lock that from the inside," Chris said, nodding his head toward the storage room door. His voice was gritty with the effort he was expending to restrain himself.

Lucy drew an unsteady breath. "No," she replied, shaking her head. "Sorry."

"Damn."

"I'll second that."

Her hazel-eyed companion studied her wordlessly for several seconds, then glanced away, his expression turning speculative. When he returned his gaze to her, she caught a glimpse of something that sent her pulse skyrocketing. Her heart skipped a beat. Or two. Or three.

She spoke Chris's name on a questioning inflection, her already agitated senses buzzing with possibilities.

He smiled slowly, the curve of his lips wicked. "Kneel up for me, sweetheart."

"But—"

"There's no reason for both of us to be frustrated." His hands settled on her hips as he spoke, compelling her to do as he'd instructed.

"I . . . don't . . ."

"Yes, you do."

His fingers splayed. He stroked her from waist to knee, then slipped his hands beneath the hem of her hopelessly wrinkled wine-colored dress. His palms curved possessively against the naked flesh just above her knees. She gasped when she realized his intention.

"*Chris*—"

"Relax, sweetheart," he counseled.

She bit her lip as he moved his hands upward. Response rippled through her, lapping away at inhibition. His touch was utterly sure and intensely sensual.

"It's . . . d-difficult to relax . . ." she managed ". . . when I can't b-breathe."

Chris chuckled, massaging the flesh of her inner thighs in an erotically insistent rhythm. "Try."

Lucy closed her eyes, beginning to feel a bit dizzy. After a moment she asked, "Do you kn-know what the . . . r-real . . . problem with our r-relationship was?"

His fingers stopped moving for a split second, then resumed their upward progress. "Aside from interfering families, a disastrous lack of communications skills, your insecurity and my blind stupidity, you mean?"

"Mmm—" she shuddered "—hmm."

He cleared his throat. "Then not offhand, no."

She opened her eyes and confronted him. "Our love-making was too . . . g-good."

This time, more than Chris's fingers stilled. His whole body seemed to freeze. He gave her a look so incredulous that she began to giggle.

"Too *good?*" he finally repeated, his voice a note or two higher than it had been. His tone suggested that he was questioning both his hearing and her sanity.

"Uh . . . hee-hee-hee . . . huh."

"This must be one of those gender things," Chris declared after a slight pause. "You know. Where men and women look at the same set of facts and come to completely different conclusions about them. Because from a guy's point of view . . . *there's no such thing as too good.*" His well-shaped mouth twisted. "Or too much, for that matter."

Lucy managed to clamp down on her risibility. The point she wanted to make was not entirely facetious.

"I've thought about this," she insisted, beginning to knead his shoulders. And she had. "No matter how bad things were between us out of bed, we could always make them up *in* it."

"And that was a . . . problem?"

She nodded, her hair shifting around her throat. "I think it kept us from discussing what needed to be discussed, Chris. It was a . . . uh . . . diversion."

"I see." He began to feather the pads of his thumbs against her skin. The caress was as deliberate as it was delicate. The muscles of her stomach contracted in quivering reaction. "So, what are you suggesting, sweetheart? The key to our making things work this time around is a commitment to celibacy?"

Now it was her turn to give him an incredulous look.

"*No!*" She wondered whether her voice sounded as breathless to him as it did to her. "Of course not. I was just, uh—" She pressed her lips together as a sudden jolt of pleasure hit her. "Making— Oh, oh!— An, uh, obser . . . vation."

"Good." A hint of masculine smugness edged the word. "Because cold showers and self-abuse aren't two of my favorite things."

"Mmm..." Lucy arched back as his hands moved up a critical inch or two. Her pulse was thumping like a crazed jackrabbit. "Doing without you doesn't exactly appeal to me, either."

"I'm flattered to hear it."

"It's fact." She inhaled sharply. "Not... flattery."

"In that case, I'm *thrilled*."

She closed her eyes as he brushed against the arousal-dampened fabric of her panties. Somewhere in the back of her mind, she was very, very thankful she'd discarded her ruined panty hose when she went to the ladies' room.

"It wouldn't be much fun," she said.

"What? Doing without me?"

"Mmm. A couple of days and I'd be wandering through the produce section of the supermarket, fantasizing about cucumbers or something."

"Lucy!"

Her lashes fluttered up. Brown eyes met hazel ones. She smiled. Chris seemed shocked. Genuinely shocked. She rather liked that.

"Big cucumbers," she clarified, in deference to his male ego, struggling to keep a straight face.

"*Lucia Annette—*"

"Jumbo ones," she quickly amended. "Or maybe, um...egg—" she broke off on a gasp as Chris edged a finger beneath the thin cotton that shielded the petaled folds of her femininity "—*plants.*"

"I know it's been ten years, sweetheart," her ex-husband said between gritted teeth. "But if you're remembering that particular portion of my anatomy as being green or purple, you're going to be in for a major surprise."

He began to caress her in earnest then, making her shift and twist and cry out. Lucy gave herself up to the acutely carnal sensations, ceding control to Chris...temporarily.

"This—" a white-hot pulse of response detonated within her "—isn't f-fair to you," she eventually protested, twining her arms around his neck.

"Don't worry." He showed his teeth in a decidedly dangerous smile. "I know you'll make it up to me."

Her pleasure-primed imagination served up several explicit scenarios for doing so. Lucy shuddered, a spiking rapture ravishing her senses. When she regained the ability to articulate, she said, "I just don't like being the o-only one— Oh. Oh, Chris—"

"Only one...what?" he asked, pushing her right to the brink with a diabolically calculated caress.

"Enjoying...m-myself."

Chris smiled again, his eyes brilliant beneath partially lowered lids. Then he leaned forward and brushed his mouth lightly against hers.

"What makes you think you are?" he inquired with silken intensity.

Lucy never got a chance to answer, because a split second after he asked the question, the man who had been her first lover triggered her release. She came apart, pressing herself against his clever fingers, clinging to his forearms with convulsive force.

"Oh...oh...*Chris*..."

He blotted out the sounds of her ecstasy with a searingly passionate kiss.

"So, sweetheart," Chris drawled a long time later, straining Lucy's softly tangled hair through his fingers. "Was it good for you?"

His ex-wife gave him a startled look. Then her ripe, rosy mouth twitched, and she started to giggle. After a moment, she buried her face against his chest in a less than successful bid to muffle her giddy laughter. Her shoulders shook. Her hilarity was punctuated by several helpless-sounding snorts.

"Lucy..."

She kept laughing.

Chris tamped down a flash of quintessentially male irritation, telling himself that she was succumbing to the strain of their ordeal. A lesser woman would have given way to hysteria hours ago—last year, in point of fact.

Still.

"Lucy," he repeated, more imperatively than the time before.

Her head came up after a second or two. Her eyes met his.

"S-s-sorry," she apologized, clearly struggling for control. "You just . . . r-reminded . . . me of something."

Chris quirked an eyebrow. "We're not back to vegetables again, are we?"

"Wha . . . ?" she began blankly. Then color flared in her cheeks. "Oh. That. No."

"Thank God for small favors."

"I thought we'd established they were *large* v-vegetables."

"Lucy!"

She gave a breathy little laugh and feathered her mouth along the line of his jaw. "Just joking."

"Yes, well, postcoital comedy can have a damaging impact on a man's ego."

"Oh, dear." Lucy shifted her position a bit, swatting a lock of hair away from her face. She gave him an up-from-under-her-lashes look that raised his internal temperature at least a degree. "Can I kiss it and make it better?"

Chris suppressed a smile. Lord, she was irresistible when she was playing fresh and feisty! "Later."

She feigned a pout.

"You can tell me what you were laughing about."

Her expression cleared. "Tina Roberts," she answered with devastating simplicity, her dimples deepening at the corners of her mouth.

Chris's pulse stuttered. "Tina . . . Roberts."

"My former maid of honor. Actually, she's Tina Palucci now."

Yes. He knew. But he wasn't sure how to tell her.

"Remembering her made you laugh?" he questioned, stalling as he tried to come up with the right words. That he was going to fess up was a foregone conclusion. He just wanted to do it . . . right.

"Something she said. It was a long time ago. We were talking about men and, ah, having sex." She paused, smiling wryly. "Or maybe I should say *she* was talking and *I* was listening with rapt—if slightly horrified—attention. Because I hadn't done it yet, and Tina very definitely had."

"So—?"

"So, she said that most men follow the same pattern after they've done the deed. First, they roll off. Then—"

"They want the woman to tell them how good it was."

"*Great*. The adjective Tina used was *great*. She also mentioned something about guys who want girls to turn into pizzas afterward, but I can't recall exactly what it was."

"Mmm."

"Anyway, when you asked me . . ." Brown eyes twinkled.

Chris nodded his understanding, then grew serious. Lucy picked up on his change of mood instantly.

"Chris?" she asked, adjusting her position.

"There's . . . something I need to tell you."

She gazed at him for several seconds, her expression serenely trusting. Then she inclined her head and said, "All right. Tell me."

"My showing up outside this building last night wasn't really a matter of chance."

She blinked. "Wh-what?"

Chris quickly related the highlights—if that was the word—of his pre-Christmas encounter with Tina.

"So, you knew I was here in Atlanta," Lucy recapped when he finished.

"Yes," he affirmed. "But not until after I started interviewing for the foundation job."

"And you decided to come looking for me last night after you got stranded."

"I called your house first." He chuckled briefly, recalling the humorous message he'd heard when he did. "I'm afraid I disappointed your answering machine. I hung up without saying anything."

"And *then* you decided—?"

He stroked her cheek. "I was going to come looking for you eventually, Lucy. It was just a case of when my head would start listening to what my heart's known for a long, long time."

"That you still...love...me." Tears glinted in her eyes.

"Absolutely." Chris waited a beat, gazing at her with an aching tenderness. Then he asked, "You're not disappointed, are you?"

She looked stunned by the question. "About what?"

"That our running into each other on what would have been our eleventh wedding anniversary can't be ascribed to...ah...ah..."

"Destiny?"

"Yes."

"Oh, I think fate must have had a hand it," Lucy disputed. "I mean, if I'd left a few minutes earlier, or you'd arrived a few minutes later..."

He smiled. "I guess some things really are meant to be."

And then they kissed again. Lightly. Lovingly. The intention was affirmation, not arousal.

Which isn't to say that Chris wasn't as hard as a pikestaff when they broke apart. Because he was. His breathing pattern, on the other hand, was decidedly wobbly.

Lucy ran her tongue over her lips, her lashes flicking down to veil her eyes. "While we're, um, *sharing*..."

He cleared his throat and forked a hand back through his hair. Once again, his gaze strayed longing toward the storage room door. There was something going on outside. He could hear it. Although exactly what "it" was was a question mark.

He brought his eyes back to Lucy's. "Yes?" he prompted.

"It's about—" Her lashes came up. So did her chin. "—Irene Houghton."

Oh, God.

"What about her?" he asked after an uneasy moment or two.

"I didn't tell you the whole truth about why I reacted so...badly...when I saw you with her."

"Lucy—"

"I know she was your first time, Chris."

His spine stiffened. His jaw went slack. He felt himself blush like an unfledged schoolboy. "H-how—?"

"Your mother."

"My mother said Irene and I—"

Lucy patted his arm soothingly as he choked off the rest of this indignant question. Although her expression was benign, something suggested that she found his obvious discomfort amusing. Enjoyable, even. Given all he'd put her through, Chris couldn't really fault her if this was the case.

"Not in so many words," she answered. "But she did make it very clear that you and Irene were a very hot item during your senior year of high school. And since you once told me you'd lost your virginity around that time..."

He'd told her—?

Oh. Wait. Yes.

Now he recalled.

Lucy had coaxed him into the admission after the first time they made love. He'd been weak. Very weak.

"Who was *your* first time?" she'd asked.

"At the moment, I can't remember anything that happened before you said the only thing you were going to want to do afterward was do it again," he'd replied, referring back to the assertion she'd made when he'd been attempting to ascertain whether she was absolutely sure she wanted to go to bed with him.

Hmm, he mused, reviewing his retort. Scratch the *very* weak. He'd sidestepped the head-on query pretty artfully if he said so himself.

"All right." Lucy had smothered a sigh. She hadn't seemed all that surprised by his refusal to kiss and tell. "Forget who. How about when?"

"You're asking for a specific date?"

"A general time frame. End of high school."

"I see," he said.

"What did Irene do after you kissed her that day?"

Gray-green eyes locked with brown ones. "You mean after she slapped me across the face?"

"She *slapped* you?"

Chris nodded once, resisting the urge to rub his jaw. Irene had been a junior tennis champ in her teens. "A clean forehand slam to the chops."

"Ouch."

"No less than I deserved."

"Then what did she do?"

"Told me to go after you."

Lucy's eyes widened. *"Really?"*

"Really." He smiled crookedly. "Irene liked you, Lucy. No. More than liked. She admired you. She said I was lucky to have you."

"This was after the slap?"

"And right before the excellent advice about going after you that I didn't follow until it was too late."

There was a pause. Then Lucy asked, "What happened to Irene, anyway?"

Chris grinned. "The last I heard, she was blissfully married with three beautiful kids and living in Boston."

"Good." The sentiment was plainly sincere. "I'm glad for her."

"And I'm glad for *us.*"

"Oh, yes." Lucy tilted her head back, raising her mouth toward his. "That, too."

He was a heartbeat away from claiming her lips when there was a knock at the storage room door. Chris cursed under his breath. They both pulled back. Lucy began fussing with her clothes and fluffing her hair.

"Chris?" It was Butch. "Lucy?"

"It's unlocked," Chris called back with conscious irony.

The door swung open. Butch Johnson plodded in. He was carrying a steaming mug of something in each hand and had two pairs of headphones slung in the crook of his left elbow. His eyes were bleary-looking and rimmed with red. His cheeks and jaw were shadowed with new beard growth.

"Is that *coffee?*" Lucy asked in a don't-quite-dare-hope voice as she clambered to her feet. Chris stood up, too, thrusting his fingers through his hair.

"Yeah," Butch affirmed, extending the mugs. "We used the agency coffee maker. Hope you don't mind."

"Oh, no," Lucy assured him, accepting the mug and taking a long, greedy gulp. "Caffeine," she declared with a fervent sigh. "Nectar of the gods."

"Thanks, Butch," Chris said as he accepted his mug. Although his words were more prosaic than his companion's, they were no less sincere. He took a sip of the rich-smelling brew.

Mmm.

Yes.

Very, very nice.

"You two doin' okay?" Butch inquired.

Chris traded glances with Lucy, then looked at the balding burglar. "We're holding up. How about you and Tom and Dick?"

"Not bad."

"You must be getting tired," Lucy observed.

"We copped a few Zs."

"That's good."

Butch's eyes shifted back and forth several times. Then he unslung the headphones.

"Here," he said gruffly, thrusting the ear protectors at Chris. "You probably ought to put these on once I leave."

Lucy paused in the act of taking another drink of her coffee. "Are you going to start drilling again?"

"Somethin' like that."

Chris found the evasiveness of this reply troubling. The oh-so-casual shrug that accompanied it didn't do anything for his peace of mind, either.

"Butch—" he began, taking a step forward.

"Everything's gonna be fine, Harvard," the other man interrupted. "Couple more hours and it'll be *hasta la vista* for us."

And with that, he pivoted away.

"Thanks for the coffee, Butch," Lucy said.

The ex-convict turned back. "One more thing. Just so's we're clear on this. We're gonna have to tie you two back up when we clear out. I know it won't be real comfortable— although I have a feeling you won't mind all that much. You'll be okay until this place reopens tomorrow morning."

Chris felt Lucy stiffen. She lowered her coffee mug, frowning. "Uh—"

"Gotta get back to work," Butch said firmly, then pivoted away again and walked out.

"Lucy?" Chris questioned once the storage room door clicked shut. "What is it, sweetheart? The prospect of our being tied up together for another twenty-four hours doesn't strike you as fun?"

"Try another four and a half *days*."

"I beg your pardon?"

"I gave everyone the rest of the week off. Gulliver's Travels is going to be closed until Monday."

"Oh . . . God."

"Sorry."

Chris shook his head. "Don't be sorry. It was a very nice thing for you to do for your staff."

"They earned it."

"Until Monday morning, hmm?"

"Unfortunately."

"I think we need to come up with an escape plan."

"Me, too. I don't suppose—" Lucy stopped, sniffing the air. "Wait. Do you . . . smell . . . something?"

Maybe he did. Maybe he didn't. But the intuition that Christopher Dodson Banks didn't really think he possessed suddenly kicked into high gear. Without really stopping to think what he was doing, he cast aside the mug and the earphones he was holding, grabbed Lucy and pulled her down on the floor, shielding her body with his own.

There was an explosion a split second later. Not a big blast. But large enough so it seemed to jar the fillings in his molars. It also caused several pieces of the storage room's plastered ceiling to break loose and fall to the floor. One chunk hit him squarely between the shoulders. He grunted in pain.

"Ch-Chris?"

"Stay down," he insisted, controlling her movements.

"What . . . what was that?"

Plaster dust filled his nostrils. He fought down a sneeze. "The reason we were supposed to put on the ear protect—"

"Lucy?" a male voice he'd never heard suddenly called. "It's me. Wayne. I got your E-mail. Is this some kind of joke?"

Twelve

The police arrived a few minutes later, pulling up in front of the building where Gulliver's Travels was located about five seconds before the Spivey brothers and Percival Johnson came charging out of it.

The suspects were too demoralized by the utter failure of their heist to try to evade arrest, much less resist it. One officer later confided to his wife that the balding one—the one some old-timer on the force had mentioned had been nicknamed Butch years before, because he sported a buzz cut in an effort to disguise his lack of hair—had seemed almost relieved to have the cuffs slapped on.

The other two had been pretty passive at first. Then they'd started squabbling with each other about which one had messed up the explosive charge they'd used. They'd been arguing so vehemently that they were loaded into separate squad cars for the trip to the police station.

Members of the local media arrived a short time after the authorities. Several TV reporters started doing "live from the scene" reports as soon as their camera crews got set up.

Lucy and Chris's exit from the building touched off a press feeding frenzy.

"How did you happen to be taken hostage?" someone yelled.

"We got lucky," Lucy said wryly, thankful that she'd been able to retrieve her black coat and shoes before coming outside. The first day of the New Year was crisp and cold. She shivered as an icy breeze fluttered beneath the hem of her coat and fingered up her unstockinged legs.

"Wrong place at the wrong time," Chris clarified, slipping an arm around her waist. Although he'd donned his trench coat, he hadn't bothered to button or belt it. Lucy thought he looked quite rakish.

"Were you frightened?" another reporter demanded.

"Of *those* three?" Chris chuckled.

"Not once we got acquainted with them," Lucy added, not wanting to give the impression they were bad-mouthing Tom, Dick and Percival. "They were very...um...well, they weren't your typical criminals."

"Are you saying you bonded with your captors?"

"I don't know that *bonded* is the right word." Seized by a sudden mischievous impulse, Lucy slanted a teasing glance at the man she loved. "Although Chris *did* lend them some money to buy pizza."

"Pizza?" There was a ripple of incredulous laughter. "What kind of pizza?"

"Not the kind you get at Falco's Pizzeria in Chicago," Chris riposted urbanely, then smiled down at his ex-wife. Lucy braced herself to be zinged, but good. "Of course, my letting them borrow money was nothing compared to Lucy's volunteering to book them the getaway of a lifetime."

"*What?*" the horde of reporters chorused.

"*What?*" the officers accompanying Lucy and Chris exclaimed.

"Oh, man, don't you know a travel-agency joke when you hear it?" Wayne Dweck groaned, his nose ring quivering at the gullibility of the press and police. He'd followed Lucy and Chris out of the building, muttering. "And what's this 'bonding' stuff? Lucy risked her life to E-mail me a message asking for help."

"Who're you?" somebody immediately wanted to know.

"My name's Wayne Dweck—"

"Spell it!" a reporter ordered sharply.

"W-A-Y—"

"The last name, kid."

"Oh. Uh, that's Dweck. *D-W-E-C-K.* I'm an assistant at Gulliver's Travels."

"Lucy! Why Wayne?"

"Why Wayne...what?" she echoed, slightly surprised she got the words out without slurring them. Weariness was beginning to set in. So, too, was a desire to be alone with Chris. Really, truly alone.

"Why did you pick Wayne to message?"

"Actually, I messaged everyone on his E-mail list."

Wayne paled. "You...you *d-did?*" he stammered. "Using the, uh...uh...you know?"

Lucy stiffened at this reaction, encroaching exhaustion giving way to alarm.

"What's the 'you know'?" one of the reporters asked suspiciously.

"Another travel-agency joke," Chris said, flashing a potent trust-me-on-this smile. "Isn't that right, ah, Wayne?"

The platinum-haired young computer whiz gulped several times, staring at Chris as though mesmerized by the force of his personality. Finally he bobbed his head and croaked, "Y-yeah."

"But—"

"Lucy!" It was Jimmy Burns's voice, coming from somewhere in the back of the gathered throng. Everybody turned.

"What did you do, Wayne?" Lucy hissed out of the corner of her mouth at her young employee.

"N-n-nothing," he muttered, a sudden blush suffusing his cheeks. "Just don't g-get upset if some, uh, g-guys from the CIA or the, uh, NSA show up, okay?"

"If some guys from the CIA or the NSA show up, I'd advise both of you to take the Fifth or plead temporary insanity," Chris counseled, sotto voce.

"Are you—are you a lawyer?" Wayne asked hopefully.

"Uh-huh. I'm also your boss's ex-husband."

"Her ex—"

"Lucy!" It was Jimmy Burns again. He'd finally elbowed his way to the front of the crowd. He flung his arms around Lucy and gave her a great big bear hug. "I turned on the TV to watch one of the parades and I saw this news story about there being an explosion in our building! I raced right down. Are you all right?"

"I'm fine, Jimmy." Lucy returned his hug, hoping she didn't smell too rank after her ordeal. "But the office is a mess."

"Oh, man." The former used-car salesman winced. "After all that money Mr. Gulliver spent on redecorating?"

"What were these guys after?" one of the reporters questioned, finally getting to the crux of the matter.

Lucy darted a glance at Chris, uncertain whether she should answer. He shrugged. "Well," she said slowly, "they mentioned something called the Red Treasure."

Dead silence.

Then, a lot of muttering. Lucy thought she heard references to gold and jewels and cash money.

Finally, one brave soul said, "Okay. I'll be the one who admits to being clueless. I've heard the rumors like everybody else. But what the heck is a Red Treasure?"

"The Red Treasure is a priceless collection of *Gone with the Wind* memorabilia," a distinctive female voice proclaimed from the back of the crowd.

"*Tiffany!*" Lucy and Jimmy cried.

"Ms. Toulouse," Wayne intoned with a lovesick sigh.

"Out of the way," Hastings Chatwell Lee IV demanded in a bourbon-and-branch-water drawl that would not have been out of place on the battlegrounds of Gettysburg or Bull Run. "My sweetie pie is comin' through."

The ranks of the press parted. Tiffany Tarrington Toulouse sallied forward with the aplomb of a Vegas showgirl. She was clad in a silvery gray coat and matching hat. Her accessories—scarf, gloves, boots and orchid corsage—were in various shades of purple.

"Hello, Lucy, dear," she said. "Hastings and I were driving out for a little New Year's Day brunch when a bulletin about your being held hostage came on the television in his limousine."

"And naturally, my sensitive darlin' had to rush right over and reassure herself of your safety," Hastings boomed.

"I appreciate the concern, Tiff," Lucy said. "But I'm fine." She paused, her gaze flicking toward Chris. "*We're* fine, actually. This is—"

"Can we hold the introductions for a minute?" one of the press crowd requested impatiently. "What was that about *Gone with the Wind?*"

Hastings turned on the individual in question, clearly intending to chastise him for his rudeness. Lucy saw Tiffany lay a restraining hand on his arm.

"It's all right, Hastings," the older woman said. "Reporters are always under deadline pressure. It makes them forget their manners."

"Is she awesome...or what?" Lucy heard Wayne ask Chris in a passionate undertone.

"Beyond awesome," her ex-husband responded with a completely straight face.

"I'm sure you all remember the renovation work that was done on certain historic buildings in the city of Atlanta in preparation for the Olympics," Tiffany said, scanning the crowd. "Well, during the course of some of that work, a cache of papers and personal items belonging to Margaret Mitchell was discovered. Given the nature of some of these items—which bears directly on the writing of *Gone with the Wind*—the family decided to hold them back for a time. Some wag nicknamed the collection the Red Treasure because of the connection with Scarlett O'Hara. And rather than let the full truth be known, the family started some rumors about jewels and bearer bonds."

The reporters started shouting questions at Tiffany. Lucy used the hubbub to turn toward Chris and whisper, "Poor Tom, Dick and Butch! What a letdown."

"I wonder if any of them has even read *Gone with the Wind*," Chris returned.

"Oh, I'm sure..." Lucy stopped as Chris grinned his scepticism. "Okay, okay," she backpedaled. "But I'll bet at least one of them has seen the movie."

"Butch."

"And maybe Dick, with Dora-Jean."

The questioning about the Red Treasure ran its course. The reporters then turned to Chris and Lucy again.

"So, what was it like?" someone asked. "Two strangers, caught up in events beyond control?"

Lucy leaned against Chris, savoring his strength and warmth. "We aren't exactly strangers," she answered.

"What do you mean?"

"He's her ex-husband," Wayne volunteered in a carrying voice.

"*Lucy's ex-husband?*" Tiffany and Jimmy cried simultaneously, turning toward Chris.

"Chris Banks," he said calmly, extending his hand. "Ms. Toulouse. Mr. Burns. Lucy's told me a lot about you."

"Well, she hasn't told us *anything* about you," Jimmy responded bluntly.

"Including the fact that she was spending New Year's Eve with you," Tiffany added, sending Lucy a reproachful look.

"Ah—" Lucy began.

"Wait a minute!" one of the reporters cried. "You two were *married?*"

"'Divorced couple reunites in hostage drama,'" another one called out as though envisioning a headline.

"Talk about ringing out the old!" someone laughed.

"Bring on the tabloids!"

"I can hear Oprah calling."

"Oprah, hell. Hollywood! This has movie written all over it."

"But only if there's a happy ending," Tiffany Tarrington Toulouse pointed out.

There was a pause. Lucy felt the weight of several dozen pairs of eyes. Then she turned to look at Chris, and the sense of being scrutinized vanished. All at once, she was alone with the man she loved.

"Well, sweetheart?" he prompted gently, his gaze very tender.

Lucy cleared her throat. "Chris and I have made a resolution."

"I thought you didn't do that anymore," Jimmy Burns said.

"I ... changed my mind."

"So, what's the resolution?" Wayne asked.

Chris took her left hand and raised it to his lips, brushing his mouth against the spot where she'd once worn an exquisite diamond solitaire and a beautiful gold band.

"Resolved ..." he began.

"... to remarry," she said.

And so Lucia Annette Falco and Christopher Dodson Banks did.

And when they did, they knew exactly what they were doing.

Which—along with sharing with each other all that was in their hearts and minds—turned out to be the key to living happily ever after.

* * * * *

The spirit of the holidays...
The magic of romance...
They both come together in

You're invited as Merline Lovelace and Carole Buck—
two of your favorite authors from two of your favorite
lines—capture your hearts with five joyous love stories
celebrating the excitement that happens when you
combine holidays and weddings!

Beginning in October, watch for

HALLOWEEN HONEYMOON by Merline Lovelace
(Desire #1030, 10/96)

Thanksgiving—
WRONG BRIDE, RIGHT GROOM by Merline Lovelace
(Desire #1037, 11/96)

Christmas—
A BRIDE FOR SAINT NICK by Carole Buck
(Intimate Moments #752, 12/96)

New Year's Day—
RESOLVED TO (RE)MARRY by Carole Buck
(Desire #1049, 1/97)

Valentine's Day—
THE 14TH...AND FOREVER by Merline Lovelace
(Intimate Moments #764, 2/97)

Silhouette®
TM

Take 4 bestselling love stories FREE

Plus get a FREE surprise gift!

Special Limited-time Offer

Mail to Silhouette Reader Service™

3010 Walden Avenue
P.O. Box 1867
Buffalo, N.Y. 14240-1867

YES! Please send me 4 free Silhouette Desire® novels and my free surprise gift. Then send me 6 brand-new novels every month, which I will receive months before they appear in bookstores. Bill me at the low price of $2.90 each plus 25¢ delivery and applicable sales tax, if any.* That's the complete price and a savings of over 10% off the cover prices—quite a bargain! I understand that accepting the books and gift places me under no obligation ever to buy any books. I can always return a shipment and cancel at any time. Even if I never buy another book from Silhouette, the 4 free books and the surprise gift are mine to keep forever.

225 BPA A3UU

Name	(PLEASE PRINT)
Address	Apt. No.
City	State	Zip

This offer is limited to one order per household and not valid to present Silhouette Desire® subscribers. *Terms and prices are subject to change without notice.
Sales tax applicable in N.Y.

UDES-696

©1990 Harlequin Enterprises Limited

COMING NEXT MONTH

#1051 TEXAS MOON—Joan Elliott Pickart

Family Men

Private investigator Tux Bishop, February's *Man of the Month*, was determined to help feisty Nancy Shatner and keep her safe from the danger that threatened her. But who was going to protect her from him?

#1052 A BRIDE FOR ABEL GREENE—Cindy Gerard

Northern Lights Brides

In a moment of loneliness, recluse Abel Greene advertised for a mail-order bride. But when spunky wife-to-be Mackenzie Kincaid arrived, would the hesitant groom get over his prewedding jitters?

#1053 ROXY AND THE RICH MAN—Elizabeth Bevarly

The Family McCormick

Wealthy businessman Spencer Melbourne hired P.I. Roxy Matheny to find his long-lost twin. But the last thing he expected was to lose his heart to this spirited beauty!

#1054 LOVERS ONLY—Christine Pacheco

Clay Landon set about winning back his soon-to-be-ex-wife Catherine—no matter the cost. But would a seduction at a secluded hideaway lead to a passionate reconciliation?

#1055 LOVECHILD—Metsy Hingle

Jacques Gaston was a charming ladies' man who couldn't commit. But when he discovered beautiful Liza O'Malley had given birth to his secret baby, could Jacques find it in his heart to become a loving father and husband?

#1056 CITY GIRLS NEED NOT APPLY—Rita Rainville

25th book

Single father Mac Ryder didn't want delicate city-girl Kat Wainwright on his land. He knew that she wasn't prepared to deal with the dangers of Wyoming, but that wouldn't keep the rugged rancher from teaching greenhorn Kat about love.

Harlequin and Silhouette celebrate
Black History Month with seven terrific titles,
featuring the all-new *Fever Rising*
by Maggie Ferguson
(Harlequin Intrigue #408) and
A Family Wedding by Angela Benson
(Silhouette Special Edition #1085)!

Also available are:
Looks Are Deceiving by Maggie Ferguson
Crime of Passion by Maggie Ferguson
Adam and Eva by Sandra Kitt
Unforgivable by Joyce McGill
Blood Sympathy by Reginald Hill

On sale in January at your favorite
Harlequin and Silhouette retail outlet.

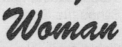